When a little learning lands a British schoolmaster a very large part in masterminding a hilarious heist, it turns into—

A FAIRLY DANGEROUS THING

"Very funny . . . a fine prescription for the blues and blahs." —*Newsday*

"Reginald Hill's sexy caper . . . is an entertainment pure and simple." —*Mike Shayne Mystery Magazine*

"EXCITING AND ENTERTAINING . . . *A Fairly Dangerous Thing* is a funny, suspenseful, off-beat novel, a rare romp among modern British manners and morals." —*The Deland Sun News*

"PLENTY OF CRISP ENTERTAINMENT." —*Kirkus Reviews*

"Outrageously enjoyable, this one." —*Oxford Mail*

"Keeps the reader gasping with laughter and fright right up to the ingenious finale." —*Publishers Weekly*

SIGNET MYSTERY

REGINALD HILL

A FAIRLY DANGEROUS THING

A SIGNET BOOK

NEW AMERICAN LIBRARY

NAL BOOKS ARE AVAILABLE AT QUANTITY DISCOUNTS WHEN USED TO PROMOTE PRODUCTS OR SERVICES. FOR INFORMATION PLEASE WRITE TO PREMIUM MARKETING DIVISION, NEW AMERICAN LIBRARY, 1633 BROADWAY, NEW YORK, NEW YORK 10019.

SIGNET TRADEMARK REG. U.S. PAT. OFF. AND FOREIGN COUNTRIES
REGISTERED TRADEMARK—MARCA REGISTRADA
HECHO EN CHICAGO, U.S.A.

SIGNET, SIGNET CLASSIC, MENTOR, ONYX, PLUME, MERIDIAN AND NAL BOOKS are published by New American Library, 1633 Broadway, New York, New York 10019

First Signet Printing, September, 1986

1 2 3 4 5 6 7 8 9

PRINTED IN THE UNITED STATES OF AMERICA

A little learning is a dangerous thing.
Alexander Pope

PART ONE

I never knowed a successful man
who could quote poetry
Frank McKinney Hubbard

CHAPTER I

Joe stood, dramatically outlined against the sky, on a rocky eminence above the Bosporus, and laughed mockingly as Cyril Solstice and Miss Onions were bound back to back (no; make that front to front, nothing was too bad for them) thrust into a sack and hurled into the swirling waters. Beside him Maisie Uppadine (or was it Maggie Cohen?) waited eagerly to reward the triumphant hero. In a sack? Why not? And front to front.

Joe sighed deeply and almost destroyed an ancient bicyclist. It was time to shake himself free from his comforting visions, especially as he was now on the main Sheffield Road and the car ahead, an ancient two-tone Consul, was moving along most erratically. This was caused in part at least, Joe surmised, by the driver's left arm being hooked over his passenger's neck. Now and then his hand seemed to make plunging motions down her front out of Joe's view, and then she would bob and twist and the car would change its speed and waver gently over the road.

Joe blew his horn as one manœuvre brought the Consul dangerously close, but this had no effect so he dropped back to a safer distance.

The glow of satisfaction his mental bout with the Pair had brought him now begin to fade, and gloomily he reviewed the actuality of the situation.

He was afraid of them, that was it, plain and simple. He, Joseph Askern, thirty-one years of age, six foot tall, darkly handsome (in a rugged kind of

9

way) with just enough hair loss to give mature distinction to a noble head, a good honours graduate, second-in-command and heir apparent of the English department, with a large responsibility allowance and little responsibility, was afraid of Cyril Solstice, Headmaster and Virginia Onions, Senior Mistress. It didn't bear thinking of.

Onions, middle-aged, huge, with a lower lip like a mantelpiece, was the more obvious danger with her one-woman war against modern degeneracy. Beside this, Cyril's obsession with the transport problems of his pupils seemed nothing. But it was his absurd insistence that all coach-bookings should be personally verified which was causing Joe to spend his lunch-hour driving into town instead of downing his usual draught of oblivion in the Bell.

Savagely he began composing another scene in which he tore the Pair to pieces.

Behind him a horn blew loudly. He came back to the surface to realize that he had halted behind the two-tone Consul at some traffic lights which had just changed to green. The cars at the front of the line had moved on, but the Consul remained still. The reason was quickly apparent. The driver had brought his other hand to bear on the situation. It was impossible for Joe to see what it was doing, but from the man's general position athwart his passenger, he surmised it was occupied on or about her upper leg.

The van behind Joe sounded again, then pulled out and overtook. Joe would have done the same, but he was too close to the Consul. He put his hand on his horn button and gave a gentle almost apologetic "peep."

Surprisingly this had some effect. The man's head rose from the woman's neck which he appeared to have been savaging with his teeth, and

he stared out of the rear window into Joe's car. Joe did not much like the look of him. It was a face which unpleasant experience seemed to have sculpted with a blunt chisel, rectangular, a single line of ginger eyebrows over long narrow eyes, a close crop of ginger-coloured hair, and a deal of pale scar-tissue round the cheekbones.

Joe smiled placatingly. The man said something to the woman who also twisted round and looked. Normally Joe would have been interested to study a face capable of generating such a fine public passion, but now he had other things to think of.

The man got out of the Consul and slowly, deliberately, made his way towards Joe's car. When he reached it, he stooped and tapped gently on the driving-seat window. He had a large gold ring inset with a bright black stone on his middle finger. It clicked once against the glass. Joe had a feeling that the man's fist would come through the window next, so he wound it down.

The face came close to his and the man spoke. His accent was local, his articulation good, his intonation quite devoid of emotion. Yet it was possibly the most menacing voice Joe had ever heard.

"Now look," said the man. "If watching pleases you, you're welcome to bloody watch; or if you don't want to watch, you're welcome to piss off. But don't blow your horn at me, lad. Get it?"

"Yes," said Joe, unwilling to trust his voice further.

"That's all right then."

As slowly as he'd come, the man returned to his own car. The lights had changed again. Hastily Joe went into reverse and backed up to give himself room to overtake. But before he could, the Consul set off and crossed the lights at red and amber.

Joe let them draw a hundred yards ahead before moving forward himself, and kept this distance. Even so he felt a sense of relief when the Consul turned right and pulled into the car-park of a large pub on the other side of the road.

The coach firm dealt quickly with Joe's query. Yes, they had the booking in hand; yes, a confirmation had been sent off the previous day, second-class mail of course, so it would probably arrive by the afternoon post. Also they were pleased to say that the detailed route mapped out by Mr. Solstice coincided almost exactly with their own preferred route to Averingerett. But it was a kind thought nonetheless.

There was just half an hour of his lunch-break left when Joe got back into his car. He turned into the car-park of the first pub he came to, dug his plastic sandwich-box out of the glove compartment and began to chew the thin edge of a ham sandwich of varying thickness. As usual he had been in a tremendous hurry that morning. His mouth couldn't quite negotiate the thick end of the wedge. Perhaps if he concentrated on the meat alone, he'd have time for a swift half. Or perhaps he should spend a couple of minutes jotting down a few notes for his lesson with the science sixth that afternoon. Cultural English! They were mad for it!

Gloomily he put down the ravaged square of bread and pulled out an old exercise-book from under the dashboard. Taking out a ball-point pen, he began to make a few notes.

The park was quite full and he would probably never have noticed the two-tone Consul if it hadn't begun to move. Not move in the normal sense that a car moves, but rather to shake. As the body shifted rhythmically on its springs, the windscreen facing Joe from the other side of the car-park caught an edge of the sun and it was this flashing effect which attracted his attention.

He watched the phenomenon with mild interest for a moment. Enviously his mind conjured up a picture of what was probably going on in the car. It was only when the shaking reached a wild climax and then suddenly went still that Joe recalled his previous meeting with the Consul's driver and decided it might be discreet to move.

He put his pen and paper down on the dashboard and turned the starter key. The starter motor let out a virile roar, the engine almost caught, then the noise died away in a plaintive whine.

He tried again with the same result.

Next time he pulled the choke full out, knowing as he did that the only result would be to flood the carburettor, but unable to stop himself as his anger at this insolent piece of machinery grew in proportion to his fear at another encounter with Squareface.

The rear doors of the Consul opened, the man got out of one side, the woman out of the other. They were both, in the words of the immortal euphemism, adjusting their dress. Despite his other emotions, Joe had time to admire their aplomb. The man indicated the pub with a movement of his head. *Post coitum torridum est*. They would probably have gone in without even looking across the park if Joe had not tried the engine once more and held the key over till the starter motor almost shook itself free of its retaining bracket.

The woman glanced over, paused, touched the man on his arm, and pointed.

The man halted, looked, said something to the woman, and began to move across the car-park. He was walking much more rapidly this time, with greater purpose.

Joe picked up his book and pen again and lowered his head, pretending to be writing. There didn't seem to be much else to do.

There was no polite tapping on the window this time. The door was wrenched violently open and a large fist with scarred knuckles gathered up Joe's shirt round his throat.

"What's your game?" grunted the man. Then his eyes fell on the book and pen in Joe's nerveless hands and his face lit up with understanding.

"So that's it!" he said. "On the snoop, eh? Couldn't they afford someone a bit better?"

"No," said Joe, half-choked, as best he could. "A mistake."

"You bet it's a bloody mistake! Listen, lad, it'll be a bigger one if you don't start talking. You'll know who I am, likely, and you'll know I don't make light promises. Right?"

"Right!" gasped Joe. It seemed the only thing to say in the circumstances.

"Good. Now we understand each other, let's have a look at what you've been putting down."

He picked up the book and began to read the jottings while Joe massaged his throat. He'll realize in a minute, thought Joe, realize his mistake. He thinks I'm a private detective! He'll apologize. *"Sorry!" I'll say. "You're sorry! Why don't you tuck your balls away and give your brains a chance?"* No, that's not so good. I'll think of something better later.

"What the hell's all this?" said the man in a markedly non-apologetic tone. "Some bloody code or something? *Two cultures? Snow? Mathematical man and the death of art?* What's it all about?"

His fist bunched menacingly once more. Joe could not take his eyes off the black-stone ring.

"They're notes for a lesson," he said, trying to

keep a tremor out of his voice. "I'm a schoolmaster. I was just making some lesson notes."

The man rippled violently through the rest of the book, glanced piercingly into the car, at the half-eaten sandwich in the plastic box, at a pile of essays on the rear window sill, at Joe's old leatherpatched sports jacket and corduroy trousers.

Suddenly he laughed. It was an unattractive noise. "Aye!" he said broadly. "I believe you. You look like a bloody schoolteacher. You poor bastard. So all you wanted to do was to watch after all, eh? You should have said!"

"I'm sorry," said Joe, not quite sure what he was sorry for but feeling an inner compulsion to preface anything he said to this man with some appeasing formula. "It was a coincidence, that's all. I just stopped for a bite of lunch."

"So did I," said the man, now full of grisly joviality, "so did I. Bloody coincidence. You should have said, lad! If I'd known it was that bad!"

He roared with laughter. Joe smiled wanly and turned the key. This time the engine burst into life at once. The man made no effort to stop him but stood back and slammed the door. He was still laughing as Joe pulled out into the traffic, though by then Joe had already thought up three good ways of putting him down and another half-dozen had suggested themselves by the time he got back to school.

CHAPTER II

Joe looked with growing amazement at Mr. and Mrs. Uppadine. Could they really be Maisie's parents? They could have passed for ninety without difficulty. No, that was an exaggeration. But the fringes of seventy certainly. They looked like each other in disguise, both small, thin, hollow-cheeked and somehow rather dusty, and they didn't seem to mind both talking at once. Joe didn't mind either. He had long since switched on the sympathetic-attentive look he reserved for parent-teacher meetings, and switched off the directional-hearing device which nature has fitted to human ears. All he got now was a general background babble as all over the school hall anxious, aggrieved and aggressive parents required advice, explanation and satisfaction of his colleagues.

The Uppadines seemed to have stopped talking. They were looking at him questioningly.

"Yes; true, true," said Joe. "How nice it is when parents take a real interest. Maisie now, she's doing fine. Fine. It's a pleasure to teach her."

He really meant it. Maisie was a splendidly developed fifteen-year-old. In one of Joe's recurring day-dreams he officiated at a black mass, using her naked bosom as a lectern. He nodded reassuringly to shake the image from his too impressive mind.

"Yes," said Mr. Uppadine. "But do you watch her, that's the thing?"

Oh God! thought Joe. She's been complaining about me staring at her breasts.

He glanced around in panic. Cyril was at the far side of the hall, but Onions was quite close, using her lower lip as a springboard to launch broadsides of damp advice at a terrified father. She seemed fully occupied, but he knew of old her capacity for taking in three conversations at once.

"It's a real worry to us," said Mrs. Uppadine. "Her being so attractive and all. We tried all we could, Mr. Askern. We kept her out of bras for a long time, but that just seemed to make things worse."

Oh yes, it would, it would, thought Joe.

"So that's why we hope you'll keep an eye on her, special like," went on Mr. Uppadine. "She's going off on some trip or other with you at weekend?"

"That's right. To Averingerett. It's a country house, eighteenth-century . . ."

"I know what it bloody well is, lad. I'm not thick."

Joe looked with new respect at this slight-figure before him. Perhaps it was not quite so incredible after all that the conjunction of these two had produced the carnal symphony which was Maisie.

"And I know what lads are. So just keep your eyes skinned when you're going around the grounds. It's a big place that. Easy to get lost in."

He nodded warningly and touched his wife on the elbow. Obediently she smiled thinly at Joe and turned away. Mr. Uppadine paused before following her. "I've had a bit of fun there meself of a time," he whispered confidentially. "You can't blame lads. So take care, eh?"

No, you can't blame them at all, thought Joe, wondering if he dared remove the name-badge in his lapel yet and drift anonymously out of the hall. He noticed that Vernon Metcalfe, the dapper little Welshman in charge of physics and his usual lunch-time drinking partner, had shed his badge and was clearly planning a break.

Vernon caught his eye at that moment and jerked his head meaningfully towards the door.

"Mr. Askern," said a woman's voice in his ear. Joe turned and his heart sank. It wasn't that he disliked the woman who stood beside him; indeed he had a great deal of sympathy with her. But her special problem was one he felt himself particularly inadequate to deal with.

"Hello, Mrs. Carter," he said with a smile. "How are you?"

Unhappy, he guessed. And with cause.

Mrs. Carter's son, Mickey, had a long history as a trouble-maker.

His only saving grace was that as he grew older he tended to stay away from school to make his trouble. The mere sight of him was enough to fill Joe with a mixture of fury and despair.

"How's Michael doing?" She always used his full name, the only person who did.

"Much the same, Mrs. Carter. When he's here, that is."

She looked at him gloomily.

"I know. I had the attendance man round again last week."

Joe was moved by her expression.

"Don't worry too much, Mrs. Carter," he said with the kind of jovial-vicar optimism he hated. "He'll be all right, you'll see. He's got some ability, you know."

"He doesn't do any work," she said flatly.

"Not homework, no. I'd have to agree with you

there. But in class now, where he's got to work, then he can reach quite a high standard."

He gave his reassuring nod, feeling a little glow of self-esteem in his belly. It was damped down immediately.

"You mean he sometimes writes things for you in class?" said Mrs. Carter, a gleam of interest on her face. "He never brings his books home. I'd like to have a look if I might, Mr. Askern. It'd be nice to see something the lad had done not too badly."

Joe pinched himself viciously through his trouser pocket. It had been a stupidly dishonest thing to say. The only piece of writing he had got out of Mickey Carter all term was at present tucked into his jacket pocket. He transferred his hand there from his trousers as though afraid that the ragged half-sheet of exercise-book paper would jump out. The class had been writing poems that afternoon. Attracted by much amusement in the vicinity of Carter's desk, he had made a sudden swoop. Mickey's muse had in the course of half an hour produced only the one immortal couplet.

> The biggest tits I've ever seen
> Belong to Maisie Uppadine.

His reward had been a sharp cuff above the ear.

Actually it wasn't bad, thought Joe. But not the kind of thing that would reassure Mrs. Carter.

"It's not so much writing I'm thinking of," he said, "as oral contribution. He asks some very penetrating questions."

Such as, "Please, sir, what's masturbation?"

Mrs. Carter's face resumed its doleful mask. She recognizes the evasions and euphemisms as well as I do, thought Joe. It's always the same for the poor woman.

Her next remark surprised him, however.

Half-turning away she said, "I'd like you to meet my husband, Mr. Askern."

Though Mrs. Carter was a regular attender of such meetings, Mr. Carter had never before been seen on the school premises. According to Joe's information, his excuse for absence was good. He had spent a great deal of his time in gaol. Whether he had some speciality in the field of crime or whether he just turned his hand to anything, Joe did not know.

"Cecil!" called Mrs. Carter sharply. Joe followed her gaze to the back of a man who was standing in a small group around Onions. He ignored the call until it was repeated. Then, with what to Joe's horrified amazement looked like a friendly farewell pat on Onions's left buttock, he turned and came towards them.

Joe would have doubted a second earlier whether anything could have ousted from his mind this nauseating vision of physical familiarity with Onions. But it disappeared as rapidly as it had flashed into awful life and was replaced by a realization just as shocking.

The man coming towards them was the man in the two-tone Consul, the one who had mistaken him for a private detective.

"Cecil," said Mrs. Carter. "This is Mr. Askern, Michael's English teacher. Mr. Askern, I'd like you to meet my husband."

"I'm pleased to meet you," he said with a broad grin, shaking Joe's hand with considerable pressure. "It's grand for me meeting all you people. I never had much education, did I, Mother? So it's nice to meet you people who know what's good for us. You do know what's good for us, don't you, Mr. Askern? And what's good for yourself?"

He eyed Joe significantly, increasing the pressure on his hand which he was still shaking.

"Oh yes," said Joe. "I hope so."

"So do I."

Carter let go of his hand and looked at his own palm.

"I think I've raised a blister, Mother. I gave that tank back there a friendly slap on the haunches and struck metal. Did you get her on a free transfer from Wakefield Trinity, Mr. Askern?"

His voice was unselfconsciously loud and Joe glanced across at Onions, fearing to be included in her disapproval at the same time as he enjoyed Carter's comments. Perhaps there was something to be said for the man after all.

"Talking of slaps, Mr. Askern, I believe you gave our Mickey a clout today. Unprovoked, he says."

"Yes, you see, well no," began Joe.

"He'd deserve it likely," said Mrs. Carter looking with stolid contempt at her husband. "If Mr. Askern judges a clout might help, then he can clout away, and welcome."

"Aye. You're probably right, Mother," said Carter cordially. "But think on, Teacher. I didn't learn much, but something I learnt was, never start owt what you can't finish."

This was spoken most friendly, with a smile and a cheerful tap with the forefinger on Joe's arm. Nevertheless Joe felt himself menaced.

"Not to worry though," Carter went on. "Mickey likes you, I think. He's looking forward to going on Saturday. Really looking forward to it."

He nodded regally as though he had just bestowed some accolade upon Joe.

Joe's heart sank. One of the few consolations about his Averingerett trips was that the trouble-makers usually had better things to do and didn't turn up. It doubled his special surveillance problems. Which was more important—to prevent Mickey from helping himself to whatever *objets d'art* he could get his thieving fingers on, or to make sure Maisie wasn't semaphoring for help with her legs in the Great Orchard?

His abstraction was noted by Mrs. Carter.

"Come along, Cecil," she said. "It's getting late and I wanted a word with the careers master."

"Over there," said Joe helpfully, pointing to a milling crowd in a distant corner. "Good night, Mrs. Carter. Mr. Carter."

"Good night," said Mrs. Carter. "And thank you."

"Watch how you go now," said Carter. "There's some wild men on the roads these days."

He waved cheerfully and set off after his wife, pausing only to administer a plainly audible slap to Onions's backside as he passed. Strangely, she didn't seem to mind, even though he turned comically towards Joe and held up his arm with the hand dangling loosely, as if broken, from the wrist.

Joe savagely ripped his badge off just as another anxious pair approached.

"Mr. Askern?" the woman said doubtfully.

"Over there." Joe pointed vaguely towards the furthermost corner of the room. "You can't miss him. He's the one who looks worried."

And not without cause, he thought, as he shouldered his way past Solstice, who unobserved had filtered right across from the other side of the room and had obviously just heard this exchange.

"Mr. Askern." He heard his voice piping behind him but he kept on going till he was safely through the door. As he stepped from the brightly-lit corridor into the deliciously cool evening, a figure came hurrying out of the shadows and almost collided with him.

"Vernon," he said, surprised. "I thought you were long gone."

"No such bloody luck. I went down to the lab, to collect some stuff. The sods have been back again. They've taken everything, including the bloody wall-clock. I'll have to tell old Sol."

"Let me get out first," begged Joe. "Onions'll probably have the staff searched before she lets them go."

Vernon didn't answer but pressed on towards the hall, looking worried. This was the third time the school had been broken into that year and it was always the labs that were worst hit. After school hours the security of the place obviously had nothing to do with Vernon, but this didn't stop the Pair from making him feel responsible. Thank God I've nothing but books in my care, thought Joe as he climbed into his little black VW beetle. And who the hell wants to steal books? None of our lot anyway!

The police'll play hell, he thought. He had met Sergeant Prince who had come to look around after the last break-in. "Useless!" he had said savagely indicating the type of window-catch used throughout the school. "Like paper knickers on a whore." His hair was prematurely white, a condition, he assured Joe and Vernon, brought about by having to deal with silly twats like Solstice and the school caretaker. (It had only taken him two minutes to sum up their own high regard for these two.)

The catches had been replaced since then, it was true. But by a type almost identical. An open invitation. Still, it was a cheek getting into the place when the hall only a few yards away was full of staff and parents. Anyone could have caught them at it.

He found he had stopped automatically outside the Bell. He glanced at his watch, uncertain whether to go in or not. This was a pub he very rarely used at night. Its main lunch-time attraction was that it was closer to the school than any other. It was unlikely he would know any of the evening drinkers and Vernon would be lucky to get away by closing time. Still, some of the others might have dropped in on their way home.

He pushed open the door marked "Saloon." Not that it mattered. The internal wall which had once separated the pub into two rooms had been knocked down some five years earlier, shortly after Joe had started teaching at the school, and if he had entered the door marked "Public" he would still have found himself in the same room. But old habits had died hard among the regulars and there was a distinct difference in atmosphere between one end of the long room and the other, although the drink cost just the same. Joe took up a position in the no-man's-land in the middle and tried to attract the barmaid's notice. At lunch-time she was always good for a chat and a bit of genteel innuendo, but now she hardly seemed to recognize him. He caught her eye but she gave him an in-a-minute nod and returned her attention to a large-scotch-and-soda in a checked waistcoat who seemed to be the acknowledged leader of the saloon end.

Joe groaned impatiently and rolled his eyes, but there was no one to complain to. Something struck him violently just below the neck.

"Well, hello again! It's Sir, isn't it? We're seeing a lot of each other, you and me, Sir, aren't we?"

He recognized the voice instantly, even felt he recognized the grip of the hand which dug tightly into his shoulder.

"Good evening, Mr. Carter," he said, trying to stop himself smiling ingratiatingly.

"Good evening to you too, Sir," said the man arching his thin ginger eyebrows to an acute angle. "Waiting for a drink, are you? Hey, Monica!"

The barmaid turned instantly, leaving the scotch-and-soda in mid-syllable.

"Hello, Cess. Same again, love?"

"That's right. And a large scotch for my friend, Sir, here."

"Oh no, a half of . . ."

But no one was listening, Joe realized. It was worse than trying to teach at half-past three on a Friday afternoon.

He found himself swept along into the depths of the public end where Cess (an apt name, thought Joe) produced a chair for him from under the rump of an uncomplaining old lady and sat him at a small round table awash with beer suds, crowded ash-trays and empty glasses. There was only one woman there among three or four men. Joe recognized her at once.

"Cynthia," said Cess. "Here's Sir. You remember Sir, don't you?"

"Oh yeah," she said peering so closely at him he felt in some danger from her long artificial eyelashes. "You was watching, weren't you? In the car-park."

She laughed and ran her tongue round her already shining red lips. Seeing her close up, dressed in a black and gold cocktail dress whose scanty material was precariously divided between top and bottom so that additional coverage for one region could only be obtained at the cost of complete indecency in the other, Joe recognized why Carter had felt it necessary to take two hands to her at the traffic lights.

Introductions of a kind were effected all round. The woman was called, according to Carter, Cynthia Hearth. One man, a squat, crinkly-haired, thick-lipped dwarf, was even more incredibly introduced as Lord Jim. None of the others was very remarkable. Joe tried to protest when he was introduced all round as "Sir," but Cess just laughed with what was evidently meant to pass as good nature. The sound made Joe shudder, so he stopped protesting and concentrated on drinking up as quickly as possible. Fearful of causing offence by drinking and leaving, he offered to buy a round. The others, who seemed to have forgotten him, looked at him in surprise.

"You're thirsty, lad," said Cess. "Lord Jim, off you go and get Sir another."

Joe began to protest.

"No," said Cess, wagging his index finger in gentle remonstrance. "You're my guest. You don't pay."

The disadvantages of this arrangement appeared when Joe, after downing his second drink, expressed a desire to be left out of the next full round and to leave.

"No, Sir," said Cess, pushing him down in his chair. "When I drink, all my guests drink."

After his third double, Joe sat meekly listening to the conversation. It seemed to be mostly about football and racing. Cynthia took little part in it, merely squirming voluptuously from time to time when Carter absently fondled her. The alcohol worked in Joe's mind and he envisaged reaching a hand under the table and stroking the inside of one of those firm, round thighs. He got as far as trying to make contact with his knees but the only reaction he got was a sharp look from Lord Jim.

He decided his directional sense was malfunctioning.

Suddenly Cess turned to him.

"Howsta doing, Sir?" he asked broadly. "What a thing it must be to have learning. What's your line, anyway?"

"English. And History. Both," said Joe, thinking the "sh" in "English" shouldn't sound quite so "shushy" as that.

"History? You're the one who's fixed up this trip to the big house on Saturday?"

" 'Sright, Averingerett."

The name of the house offered no difficulty. He could say it in his sleep. Just as he could practically walk round the place in his sleep.

"It's my specialty," he explained. "Special interest."

Cynthia yawned pointedly but Cess ignored her.

"Tell us about it," he said.

Joe had a double interest in Averingerett, northern home of the Trevigore family who had clung ferociously to their possessions despite descending into comparative insignificance a good two centuries before most of their peers.

First, it provided him with a very reasonable topic to fill in the odd period of bottom-stream history he got landed with term after term. A couple of visits a year kept him out of a whole entanglement of weekend sporting duties.

There was another more important reason. For over three years with a growing lack of interest he had been writing a Ph.D. thesis on Shelley's philosophy. One day Laidlaw, the head steward at Averingerett, who had become a good friend, offered to show him over the private part of the house. Particularly interesting had been the Book Room, a small, very pleasant relative of the Grand

Library in the public sector. Idly Joe had plucked
from the shelves a copy of Godwin's *Political Justice*
(an odd tome to find in such aristocratic surround-
ings) and had been struck to find its margins full
of comments in an almost illegible hand. But his
interest became feverish speculation when he turned
to the fly-leaf and found no name but a rough
sketch of a lake and boat, with mountains in the
background. Leigh Hunt, Shelley's friend and fre-
quent companion, had somewhere noted the poet's
habit of ornamenting his own or borrowed books
with just such doodlings. If the annotations *were*
Shelley's it was a tremendous find. And one he
would certainly not be allowed to get his hands
on.

He had told Jock Laidlaw in very general terms
that some of the volumes in the Book Room would
be a great help to him in his work and the steward
had willingly agreed to take Joe along to the room
whenever it was convenient. But he wouldn't permit books to be taken away. This meant it was
very slow work transcribing the marginalia even
though he visited the house, both with and without school parties, as often as possible. But a little
delay seemed a small price to pay for academic
immortality.

Drunk though he was, he did not feel it would
serve any purpose to explain all this to his present
audience. Instead he gave them a version of his
pre-visit pep talk.

"A great house," he said. "Great. Great. But built
on cruelty and greed, ruthless exploit ... er ...
exploitation of near-slave labour. You and me. Our
anshestors. So that a few ... *bastards*, yes, bastards could live in luchshury."

"Aye, but," said one man suddenly interested,
"they were different, them what'm-you-call-it,

Trevigores. Aristocrats. Sommut to look up to. They've got t'breeding. Not like some o' these jumped-up twats that made their brass on black market in t'war. I could name a few round 'ere. Aye."

He nodded and others nodded with him.

"But that's just what the Trevigores did!" cried Joe, excitedly banging the table. "Jus' that. They were your jump up twatsh of the Hunnerd Years War!"

He made a large gesture, depositing three or four glasses in Lord Jim's lap. The squat little man bunched an enormous fist. Cess shook his head.

"Time for beddy-byes, Sir," he said standing up. "Give us a hand there, Jim. Open car, Cyn, there's a lass. I reckon we'll have to take him home. It wouldn't look good, schoolteacher been done for d. and d."

He laughed raucously.

The night air sobered Joe up for a moment as he was half-dragged past his VW towards the old two-tone Consul. He wondered what Carter had done with his wife. Let her walk home while he went off to meet his lady love? Cyn. Cess and Cyn! What a pair!

He began laughing.

"Chuck him in the back," said Cess.

"He's not going to be sick, is he?" asked Cynthia.

"No, no," assured Joe, falling across the back seat. Then he decided he might have been premature and lowered his head gently on to an old travelling-rug which was lying loosely over something hard. He fumbled with the rug, trying to fold it over to increase the softness. It slid to the floor and he leaned down to retrieve it.

In the light of a passing sodium lamp he saw without interest what it was he had been lying on.

It wasn't until six o'clock in the morning after a night disturbed by a succession of nightmares and visits to the bathroom that he sat up in bed, suddenly and painfully, and wondered what the wall-clock from the physics laboratory had been doing in the back of Cess Carter's car.

CHAPTER III

Despite the outcries of his social conscience (which in any case was only strong enough to excite him to argument, never action) the sight of the great grey western façade of Averingerett, looped by the winding river and made mellow by the afternoon sun, always sent a thrill of pure delight along Joe's spine.

It was the second he had had that day. The first had been occasioned by the arrival at the coach of Maisie Uppadine. He had not yet grown accustomed to the incredible aesthetic changes she brought about in the drab school uniform. But today she was in civvies, orange hipster slacks and a simple white sun-top, which made no pretence of meeting at her midriff.

His pleasure here, however, had been shortlived. Despite Cess Carter's assurances at the PTA meeting, Joe had not really been convinced that Mickey Carter would turn up. Surely the thousand and one other Saturday afternoon attractions which usually kept the yobbos away would work their melancholy charm on the boy? But no. Round the corner he had come, dressed with a kind of hideous dapperness in a very light grey double-breasted suit.

"Nice to see you, Mickey," said Joe, hoping the lad had come merely to mock. But he swung himself casually aboard, saying gloomily as he did so, "Dad said I had to."

"Did he now," said Joe, hearing with pleasure

Maisie's mocking squeal at the sight of Mickey's finery. Fortunately the Saturday-afternoon-drop-out-law seemed to be applying itself in the case of most of Mickey's cronies and he had hastily instructed the bus-driver to set off.

On the drive to the house, the familiar beauties of the countryside had failed to grip him. Why, he wondered, was Cess Carter so keen on Mickey's attendance today? Some kind of warning? Perhaps. He had decided to decide he was wrong about the clock. Coincidence. Such old-fashioned, wood-encased timepieces weren't all that uncommon. But a little silent film-sequence kept on forming and running through his mind in which Mickey Carter tiptoed down the lab corridor, opened the door with a master-key (entry *had* been through the door, he had established in casual conversation with Sergeant Prince—Sol and Onions were dropping large hints that Vernon had left it unlocked) and, having filled his swag-bag or whatever he used, the boy then opened a window and gently deposited the loot in the flower-bed behind the row of cars parked there by parents attending the meeting. Perhaps Carter's car had been under that very window. Then the lad left casually, openly, wandered round to the car-park and dropped the stuff, clock and all, on to the back seat of the old Consul, covering it up with the travelling-rug. All this in daylight, or at least early dusk.

Part of him had wanted to run this little mental film through in front of Sergeant Prince. Just a very tiny part of him, but nonetheless he was proud of it. The majority, however, had been for silence and he was nothing if not a democracy. It was only suspicion after all. And it would not do for Cess Carter to think he had been talking to the police about him.

He resolved to put the whole matter out of his mind and concentrate on preventing Mickey from finding an opportunity to widen still further the gap between Maisie's slacks and her sun-top. Unbidden, the boy's couplet came to his mind.

> The biggest tits I've ever seen
> Belong to Maisie Uppadine.

It wasn't bad, really. Not bad at all. Almost unconsciously his mind began to search for a pair of follow-up lines.

A large image was needed, something metaphysical.

> . . . belong to Maisie Uppadine.
> From Manchester to Marrakesh
> That peaked and promontory flesh
> Runs its pale coral into seas
> Of sunken hopes and reveries

"Please, sir! I can see it. I can see it! Is that it?"

Startled he awoke out of the creative fit. It was little Molly Jarvis, who loved him.

"Yes, Molly," he said, looking out of the window at Averingerett. "That is it."

Surprisingly he found he had no trouble at all in keeping an eye on Mickey Carter. On the contrary, the boy seemed to be constantly under his feet as they made their way down the long corridors and through the superbly proportioned rooms of the great house. There were no official guides, just a series of strategically-placed stewards whose function was to answer questions and ensure no one approached too near the treasures on display or trespassed into the apartments still occupied by

Lord Trevigore and his large family. The stewards all knew Joe and greeted him familiarly.

"Back again, Mr. Askern? Thinking of buying the place, are you?" was a typical example of their razor-edged wit.

Joe made little attempt to keep his party together as a party. The preparatory work they had done together in class ensured, in theory anyway, that the children had some familiarity with the house. They each had special assignments concerned with a variety of aspects of the visit, and the route round the building was well signposted and, more important, stewarded. So Joe merely answered the questions of those near to him, never at very great length. He had discovered very early in his visits that anything resembling a lecture not only alienated his own pupils but attracted a little crowd of casual tourists who stuck close to him for the next half-hour.

Even this might have been preferable to Mickey's attentions.

"Please, sir, are them books real?" In the library.

"Please, sir, what's that silver worth?" In the Banqueting Hall.

"Please, sir, are them paintings or photos?" In the Long Gallery.

He had a grubby little notebook (they all did, but Mickey's was twice as grubby as anyone else's) in which he noted Joe's answers with a blunt stub of pencil.

It was a relief to pass via the greenhouse, where the Great Vine clung tenuously to life like an aged relative in an intensive-care unit, into the garden.

"Please, sir."

It was Maisie this time, so Joe gave her the full attentive-teacher bit.

"Is this *all* the garden?"

She made a naturally graceful, all-inclusive gesture, obviously thinking of the patch of yellowing lawn over which her dad trundled his well-kept mower once a week.

Joe looked round at the level lawns, the fountained lake, the cascade, the carefully positioned groves, and to the east on the rising ground running up to the line of trees which marked the boundary, the great areas of parkland over which sheep grazed and across which the Trevigore hunt had for many centuries established man's right to seigniorage of the animal kingdom.

"Yes, Maisie," he said. "That's the garden."

He looked around at his flock, suddenly warming to them. This lot didn't give a bugger for the Trevigores. They were going to run wild around this egocentric rearrangement of nature by some eighteenth-century chinless wonder. They were going to eat bloater-paste sandwiches in his rose-garden, carve their names in his arboretum, and probably piddle in his cascade. It was a kind of justice.

"Right!" he called. "Everyone here? All got your sandwiches? Now off you go and have a look round the gardens. Remember, nothing, practically nothing, you see is where it is by *chance*. Someone put it there. Enjoy your picnic, don't make a mess. And back here at four-thirty sharp. Right here!"

He pointed dramatically at the naked wrestler beneath whose marble menaces they stood. The children set off merrily, happy to be out in the sunshine. Mickey came up to Joe and grinned insinuatingly.

"Hey, sir," he said, jerking his head at the statue. "What a little one he's got, eh?"

"Go and eat your sandwiches, Carter," said Joe wearily.

He himself turned and made his way back toward the house hoping to find Jock Laidlaw and perhaps even pay a quick visit to the Book Room.

Today he was disappointed; seated behind the steward's desk was a man he didn't know.

"Hello," he said. "I was looking for Jock, Mr. Laidlaw. Is he about?"

"No," said the man uninvitingly. "He's sick."

"Oh dear. Nothing serious, I hope?"

"No."

Obviously there was little to be got out of this fellow. Not even a chat, which was a pity. He liked to be kept up to date on what was going on around the place. There'd been some activity he noticed up along the ridge to the east and he'd wondered if perhaps the Blue Grotto was finally being reopened. A small complex of rather pretty caves, it had been designated as dangerous after a rock-fall the previous year and closed to the public since then.

"Give him my regards if you see him. Mr. Askern, tell him. Cheerio."

He received no reply and was happy to get out into the sunshine again. It was now very warm and after five minutes he abandoned his plan of walking up to the Blue Grotto to see for himself and cast around for a shady spot in which to eat his pork pie and apple. He felt miserable. You're getting old, Joe Askern, he thought. Old and pathetic.

What you want to solve all your problems is a rich luscious bird.

Mentally he checked through his availability list. Even including one or two who would not have got on a remote-possibility list two or three years earlier, there weren't many. Really only two worth considering at all.

There was Maggie Cohen in the domestic science

department. She was all right, Maggie. But he was
reluctant to get too involved with another teacher.
Most of his friends in the profession had married
other teachers. There was something nasty about
it. A husband's profession ought to have a certain
status, a certain mystique in the eyes of his wife.
This was plainly impossible when they both did
the same thing. Besides, his old mother in her
pensioner's flat in Chingford would start the third
world war if he brought home a girl called Cohen.
It had taken her half a lifetime fully to accept that
his father came from north of Luton.

That left Alice Fletcher, just on the turn from
bachelor girl to spinster, who had the flat beneath
his. She was willing, there was no doubt about
that. But she had the great disadvantage of being
flat-chested. Hardly a contour in sight. Perhaps
the daily apparition of Maisie had set up a block of
some kind. But a man had to set some limits and
thirty-six inches was his. Anything below was out.

Which left him with nothing but a pork pie and
an apple. He fancied neither and instead went to
sleep, dreaming uneasily of an old age of golf and
the local Poetry Society.

The rest of the visit passed uneventfully. He scru-
tinized Maisie carefully for any sign that she had
"had an experience" as his mother used to call it,
but she looked much the same as before.

What the hell do I expect? he wondered gloomily. A little red light to start winking in her navel?
Christ, she's over fifteen. Another few months and
it'll all be legal anyway.

But he remembered the anxiety on her parents'
faces and resolved to have a chat with Maggie
Cohen. Onions was officially in charge of sex education (which was like making General Booth land-

lord of a pub) but it was to Maggie the girls turned. She'd be able to say if Maisie was fully kitted out.

He spent a quiet evening, spoilt only by two encounters with Alice Fletcher. During the first, he refused her invitation to supper with her on the grounds that he'd just eaten. During the second, no words were spoken as they passed in the hall, Joe vainly trying to conceal the bag of fish and chips he had just purchased.

The following day dawned bright and warm and Joe forswore his original plan of lying in bed with the papers in favour of going down to the golf club. He had only been a member a few weeks, Vernon having finally egged him on to join on the grounds that he needed someone there he could beat. It was as good a place as any to have Sunday lunch.

He got changed and lingered in front of the locker-room wondering whether to wait till some other partnerless soul turned up or to strike out by himself. It would be a slow business on a Sunday, and lone players weren't very popular.

"Well by Christ, it's Sir! How's your head, eh? By God, you were rough!"

His heart sinking, Joe turned to look at Carter.

"Good morning, Mr. Carter."

"Cess, lad. Cess. You can't mister a man as has put you to bed."

"Yes. Well. Thanks very much. It was kind . . ."

"Not at all. Least we could do. Cyn saw you safely tucked up. The woman's touch, though you weren't in a state to appreciate it!"

Carter was wearing all the gear. Immaculate blue shirt with matching slacks. Brown and white calf shoes. A bright orange cap with a long peak. And there was something more than a hundred pounds' worth of equipment on the trolley behind him.

Uneasily Joe shifted on his shoulders the second-hand bag containing six ancient clubs.

"How'd you know where to take me?" he asked.

"Looked in your wallet. You didn't notice? Now then, Lord Jim'll be pleased about that. He prides himself on his touch. You waiting for someone?"

"No. I just thought . . ."

"Let's join up then! That is if you don't mind. Sir versus Cess! The match of the decade. Right?"

"Well, all right."

Carter was all smiling bonhomie as they walked to the first tee, but it didn't dispel the feeling of unease, almost fear, Joe felt whenever he was near the man. He was also trying to piece together the uneven kaleidoscope of appearances that he presented. Layabout lecher, having it off in a pub car-park at lunch-time; working-class father, proud of his son's toughness, letting his mother do the worrying; hard drinker, obviously respected (if that was the word) in the pub circles he moved in; and now, unexpectedly, golf club member, expensively equipped, expansively mannered.

Add to that the threat of physical violence Joe felt emanating from the man and the recent suspicion of criminal involvement, and you were left with a character to be wary of.

He seemed to know most of the people they met, exchanging greetings with an unforced joviality.

"How long have you been a member Mr. Car— Cess?" asked Joe.

"Me? Oh, a while. A while. Nice shot, lad!" he said admiringly to the man who had just driven off the first tee by which they were waiting. "On you go, Sir. I'll give you the honour."

"I'd prefer that you didn't call me 'Sir,'" said

Joe, quietly, hoping that his voice didn't really have a tremor in it. "The name's Joe."

"Joe, eh? Sir Joe! You and Lord Jim, you'd make a pair!" He roared with laughter, then his manner changed and he touched Joe on the shoulder. "Right you are, Joe. Joe it shall be."

He nodded as though bestowing an accolade.

"Morning, Mr. Askern," said a voice behind them.

"Why, hello, Sergeant Prince," said Joe to the ludicrously white-haired man who had just come down from the clubhouse.

"Morning, Sergeant," said Cess. "Come to check that we don't drive too fast?"

"Not much chance of that on a Sunday," said Prince evenly. "I think you can go now, unless you hit like Nicklaus."

Joe teed up and drove off, saying a little prayer of thanks as the ball went straight down the fairway.

"Half a quid suit you?" said Carter as he addressed the ball.

"All right," said Joe, wishing almost immediately he hadn't spoken as his opponent's ball flew effortlessly down the fairway and came to rest a good sixty yards beyond his own.

This was the pattern of the game and soon Joe was a couple of holes down. It was very slow progress as there were a lot of people on the course and they had to wait at nearly every shot till those ahead were out of range.

"My lad enjoyed his visit," said Carter during one such wait.

"I'm glad."

"Made him respect learning a bit. If you know nowt, you are nowt, I tell him. He were very impressed by all you knew, Joe."

"Really?"

"Yes. Very. You'll have a few books about yon place, I expect?"

"Averingerett? Yes. One or two. Why?"

Carter looked faintly embarrassed, an emotion which did not sit well on his brutally moulded features.

"I just wondered if you'd mind lending them to our Mickey. He's really interested. I'd see he took good care of them."

Joe felt slightly touched. And very incredulous.

"Well, if you think so . . . of course, I'd be pleased to."

"Thanks, Joe. I think they're off the green now. We can play our seconds."

As far as Joe was concerned they could have played their second shots much sooner. The chances of his reaching the green were very remote.

He addressed his ball. There was a thump behind him and looking round he saw a ball rolling down the fairway towards them. The tee behind was out of sight over a rise and you played your tee-shot at a marker-post.

"They must have thought we'd have gone on by now," said Joe, puzzled to see his partner's face so flushed.

"Bloody pigs," said Cess between set teeth. "Bastards think they can do what they want."

He strode up to the ball and trod on it violently, sinking it deep into the turf.

"Let's see 'em get out of that," he said, then with an odd glance at Joe, "Not a friend of yours, is he?"

Joe was glad to lose at the fourteenth and suggested that they shouldn't bother to finish the round but walk in.

"I'll play a couple more," said Carter, glancing at his watch. "My Yorkshire pud's still in the oven."

"How is Mrs. Carter?" asked Joe casually.

"Grand. Champion. You must come and have a bite with us some time, Joe. She'd like that."

With Cynthia to make up a four, wondered Joe as he trudged back to the club-house.

On an impulse after lunch he telephoned Maggie Cohen's number but could get no reply. Reluctant to go back to his lonely flat and unable to face the traditional husband and wife Sunday afternoon foursome, he went for a walk by the river.

Christ, he thought gloomily, if I stop enjoying Sundays I'll start looking forward to Mondays and end up like Cyril and Onions. At least Cyril's got a wife and family. Perhaps he's a different man at home. My trouble, he mused, peering into the muddied depths of the foam-pustuled waters, is that I'm the same man everywhere. Not a sign of life down there, dead, all dead of industry. Me too if I'm not careful. Someone somewhere's got my share. Trevigore, Lord bloody Trevigore, that's who it is, among others.

Trevigore's got my share.

He must have spoken the words out loud for two young women with prams looked round startled, and Joe walked away, blushing guiltily.

I'll be exhibiting myself next, he muttered, noting that even his mutter attracted the attention of a passing matron. That's how I'll end up. Murky depths of a dead middle age.

But as he passed over the small wooden bridge which would lead him from the dangerous atmosphere of the municipal park, he glanced once more at the river and saw a bright silver shape rise momentarily to the surface, devour a fly, and then head downstream with a flick of its tail.

Filled with new hope (he was a great believer in

signs) he resolved to go home and have it away with Alice Fletcher, even if it meant marrying her.

Fortunately perhaps, Alice was out, so he spent the evening marking hideously dull compositions, his only concession to the call of the senses being the continuation of the Maisie-poem.

He fell asleep in his chair trying to think of a rhyme and woke with a start at two o'clock in the morning, knocking the pile of exercise-books to the floor, and with an odd feeling that someone had been trying the door of his flat.

CHAPTER IV

As though in reaction against the depressions of Sunday, the week began very well. Onions was absent for a start.

"Pregnant," asserted Vernon, looking significantly in the direction of Joe. "Or kidnapped. If we don't pay ten thousand quid by the end of the week, they'll send her back."

"She's having a mouth transplant," claimed Joe. "At Whipsnade. From a hippo."

"God, you're all terrified of her, aren't you?" said Maggie Cohen. "Otherwise you wouldn't be so nasty."

Maggie Cohen was a big happy girl who stopped just short of being jolly. At twenty-four she saw no reason in the world to be afraid of anyone, not even the Onions-Solstice juggernaut. Only seven years younger than Joe, she sometimes appeared to him like a new kind of human being. When this feeling came on, he usually invited her out for a large Chinese meal and attempted to establish some kind of fingerhold on her round, luscious breasts. An evening of such good-natured skirmishing reassured him once more of her essential humanity, as well as giving a little necessary airing to his mammary obsession.

The truth about Onions turned out to be more absurd than the scurrilous rumours. She had been summoned for jury-service at the assizes where the main case as far as local interest was concerned was *Regina v Thomas Chubb*, Retail Chemist and, till recently, Alderman.

Chubb was accused of a complex of offences arising from his alleged enthusiasm for taking obscene photographs and ciné-films which he sold and rented in (it was rumoured) some very influential local circles. The offence had been brought to light by the use he was alleged to have made of certain expensive pieces of photographic equipment purchased by the council for the municipal museum and art gallery.

"It'll be the death of her!" said Vernon. "She won't know which way up to hold the pictures!"

"Watch your trousers when she comes back, lads!" cackled Colley, the ancient head of chemistry. "She'll have seen what she's been missing."

"Poor old Chubb," mused Joe. Maggie Cohen smiled at this display of human sympathy.

"Perhaps his counsel will have the sense to object," she said.

The reappearance of Onions herself after morning break seemed to put an end to the business until she let it out that she was merely temporarily released and had to reappear later in the week. She implied that the judiciary were getting the dross out of the way first and saving both Chubb and herself for a grand finale, an opinion which, as far as Chubb was concerned, the papers substantiated.

"Poor old Chubb," said Joe once more, hoping for more approval from Maggie. It was like a light turning on behind her eyes when she directed her full, gift-wrapped smile specially at you. She did it now and he asked her on the spot to go out with him that evening, thanking his lucky stars Alice Fletcher had been out the previous night. Her acceptance more than compensated for Onions's return and he went about his business with a light heart.

Even the children seemed particularly well-behaved. The Carter gang gave him no trouble at all and when Mickey approached him at lunch-time, Joe greeted him with unusual amiability.

"Please, sir," said the boy. "My dad says you said you'd lend me some books."

"Did I?" said Joe.

"Yes. About that house."

"Averingerett? Oh yes, of course. You enjoyed your visit then?"

"Yes. It were grand," said Mickey without a great deal of enthusiasm.

"I'm pleased. Look, I'm sorry but I forgot about the books and they're mostly at home. I'll try to remember tomorrow. OK?"

Surprisingly the boy held his ground.

"My dad said I were to read them tonight."

"Did he now? Can't you read them tomorrow night then?"

"I'm busy tomorrow night," said Mickey, then as an afterthought, "I'm busy every night but tonight."

"Lucky you," said Joe. He found Mickey's sudden desire to read difficult to believe and normally his reaction would have been to send the lad packing. But his own rare state of contentment, plus a memory of a pair of thinly-slitted eyes boring into him from under the line of ginger eyebrows, made him say, "Well, if you care to call in at my flat after school, I'll dig 'em out for you. You know where I live?"

"Yes, sir."

The yobbos always knew where you lived, as a constant stream of football pools and other un-wanted literature attested, plus, if you were very unlucky or unpopular, bangers through the letter-box on Guy Fawkes night and cracked window-panes any night of the year.

The rest of the day passed pleasantly. Despite the fact that Joe had a car and didn't linger around the staff-room much after four o'clock, Mickey was already waiting for him outside his flat.

"Wait there," said Joe firmly as he opened the door. He could think of half a hundred reasons right off why he didn't want the likes of Mickey Carter crossing his threshold. Indeed he had some misgivings as he selected three fairly expensive tomes from his shelves. Only one of them was specifically about Averingerett, but the others contained substantial sections on the house.

He explained this carefully to the boy on the doorstep and also stressed the good condition of the books and their value.

"Yeah," said Mickey nodding. "Yeah."

"I must be mad," said Joe as he listened to the boy's feet clattering away down the stairs.

Anyway that's my good scholastic deed for to-day. Oh ye patron saint of frustrated pedagogues, take note and smile on me tonight. For tonight with your kind help, I intend to score.

He selected one of his old Judy Garland records and put it on the turn-table, starting it revolving as he went into the shower. The young girl's voice, incredibly vulnerable, incredibly mature, talked and sang her undying affection for Clark Gable.

"You made me love you," sang Joe.

An even more discordant noise penetrated the stream and he trotted naked across his bedroom to open the window. A small black and white cat with a reproachful look on its face stepped off the sill into the room.

"Where the hell have you been, Vardon?" asked

Joe, but received no answer. The cat was rolling on its back by the record-player. Vardon was an even more enthusiastic Garland fan than Joe.

"Yoo-hoo!" called Alice from the little patch of communal garden below in which she was hanging out some bits of washing.

What's she doing back from work so early? wondered Joe starting back from the window, conscious suddenly of his uncovered manhood.

"I didn't wanna do it, I didn't wanna do it," sang Garland.

"Miaow," said Vardon.

Joe returned to the shower, only to be brought out of it again two minutes later by a ring at his doorbell.

"You couldn't let me have a jug of milk," smiled Alice. "Oh, I'm sorry. I didn't realize you were having a bath. I'll come back, shall I?"

"No. Wait," said Joe. He returned from the kitchenette with a pint bottle.

"That's far too . . ."

"Take it," said Joe. "I'm out tonight so I won't be needing it."

Jesus, he thought as he towelled himself. If the sight of my naked shoulders brings them running, what's the rest of my torso going to do?

Seriously, Alice could be a problem, he told himself smugly. She's just too accessible. And I'm too vulnerable! He turned the shower to cold. "Put your arms around me, honey," sang Garland and his mind turned to Maggie.

Now there was a girl worth serious consideration. Perhaps if he said it quickly enough, his mother would think she was called *Coon*. Which was probably worse. Surely, though, one minute of Maggie's charm would dissociate her in his mother's mind from archfiends like Allie Cohen who ran the betting shops in Ilford?

In any case, he said to himself, it matters not if mother does not like it. For, as the good book states, mother is not going to get it.

Even Vardon's derisive grunts could not undermine his sudden optimism.

Tonight was the night!

Maggie's strength, he decided later as he let himself back into the flat, lay in the amiable way she refused. There was nothing absurdly moral or frigid about it; her refusals didn't bring the evening to a cold, uncomfortable end. She accepted as perfectly natural and even enjoyable his efforts to get among her underclothes, and turned the whole thing into a highly entertaining wrestling match where there was always the hint that some day Joe might win. He hadn't yet, but the memory of the evening just past was very pleasant for all that.

They had gone to an Indian restaurant. Joe had lost his faith in the Chinese and Vernon had long been assuring him of the aphrodisiac qualities of Bombay Duck. Indeed as far as Joe was concerned it worked perfectly, though perhaps sitting knee to knee with Maggie in the darkly-lit, exotically perfumed booth helped.

Halfway through the meal a group of people had come into the restaurant talking with that loud certainty of their own standing shared only by the public schools and Yorkshire businessmen. Loudest of all was a little round man with a shiny black moustache that looked as if it had just been painted on.

Maggie's foot dug into Joe's calf, too violently for even the greatest optimist to assess the intention as erotic.

"Ugg," she said through a mouthful of Vindaloo prawn.

"It's probably the lime-pickle," said Joe sympathetically.

"No! Chubb!" whispered Maggie swallowing and reaching for her glass of iced lager. "That's Chubb. You know. *Onions's* Chubb."

"Good Lord! But I thought he was locked up?"

"He'll be on bail, fool."

Joe tried to glance discreetly round at the group of men but they had seated themselves in a booth out of his line of vision.

"Are you sure? How do you know?"

She giggled, a lovely bubbly sound.

"No, I'm not one of his models, if that's what you're thinking. I've seen his picture in the paper, that's all."

"What was he doing? Hanging naked from a chandelier?"

She kicked him again.

"I've never seen the point of that."

"What?"

"Everyone says it. About hanging naked from a chandelier, I mean. But why? I mean did anyone ever *do* it?"

"Oh yes," assured Joe in his serious lit-crit. voice. "That's why all these stately homes are full of chandeliers. You should see Averingerett. Can't move for them."

"I'd like to some time. I've never been."

"Good God," said Joe. "Not really?"

"Can I have this last prawn? No, really. They say you've been a hundred times. Is that right?"

"Not quite. But once or twice, yes."

"Why? Are you eating this onion pickle as well? Good; it doesn't matter if we both eat it."

"What doesn't matter?" he asked lasciviously.

"Why do you keep on going back to Avering-gerett?" she insisted.

"Well, it's easy," he said. "I don't have to think about it. No, I suppose it's a kind of love-hate relationship really. I love the place as an artifact, as something created by a certain kind of comprehensive artistic vision. At the same time I resent it and what it has stood for in history. I suppose I feel that helping to defeat that every time I lead my little crocodile of kids through the main doorway. It's a kind of snook-cocking. But I still feel we're the defeated ones as we gawk helplessly at that great dining-table loaded with porcelain and silver that the likes of us can never use. Or look at those rows upon rows of books in the library. I'm damn sure not a Trevigore touches them from one year's end to another."

He fell silent and Maggie took his hand in one of hers, spooning the rest of her curry into her mouth with the other.

"You sound as though you'd like to see the stuff shared out amongst everybody. It wouldn't go far!"

"I suppose I would in a way," he said. "At least it'd go a bit farther than it has done."

She pushed her plate away.

"There now. You can tell me what all these odd-sounding sweets mean."

On their way out, he glanced back once more in an effort to see Chubb and this time was successful. He looked quite a nice little man, the kind of chap you wouldn't mind approaching for something very *personal* as he stood in his white coat behind the counter of his chemist's shop. Poor bastard.

He turned and walked into Lord Jim. It was like walking into a wall.

"Sorry," gasped Joe.

Lord Jim showed no sign of recognition or acknowledgment and went on into the restaurant.

"That was lovely," said Maggie leaning into him outside the door, and he forgot instantly all about Chubb and Lord Jim. Maggie was right. If you'd both been eating onion pickle, it didn't matter.

Vardon thought differently, however, sniffing his breath with disgust and refusing to sleep on the bed beside him. Joe didn't care. It had been a good night and the wrestling match had gone to the last three falls before he lost. He smiled. There had been a moment in the final round when he thought he was going to get a submission. Vardon changed his mind and jumped back up on the pillow. Nothing was impossible.

Smiling, he fell asleep.

The rest of the week continued under the same fair skies that had ushered it in. At school the children seemed bent on demonstrating their usually deep-hidden capacity for good behaviour, Onions was too concerned with the possibility of talking a jury into flogging Chubb to bother with Joe's minor misdemeanours, and Maggie seemed to have let their relationship move on to another stage. His imagination worked overtime on this.

At home, things were well too. Alice had suddenly been summoned away to nurse her sick father, thus putting a constant temptation out of the way and also leaving the place to Joe alone, as the couple who occupied the topmost of the three flats into which the old terraced house had been converted were away on holiday. It was a comfort to think he could bring Maggie back here on Friday without the worry that Alice was going to come trotting up the stairs in search of a cup of sugar or half a loaf of bread.

Not that there was any certainty that Maggie would come up, but he had high hopes. Vardon was the bait, Maggie having displayed great interest when Joe told her about the cat.

"You're my etchings, Vardon," said Joe, tickling the little animal's upturned chin. "Be charming or you'll miss your bacon rind."

Friday arrived with still no flies in the ointment. Maggie greeted him warmly in the staff-room before assembly.

"All right for tonight?"

"You took the words out of my mouth," he said.

"You never know where they've been," she smiled. "Hey, seen the paper? Someone's got the same idea as you, try to spread the Trevigore wealth around a bit."

"What?"

"Here. Look." She showed him a small paragraph in the *Telegraph*. It stated that an attempt had been made to enter Averingerett, Lord Trevigore's northern home, the previous night. An alarm had gone off and the would-be burglars had retired empty-handed. That was all.

The mention of Averingerett reminded him of the books he had loaned to Mickey Carter and he tackled him at break. He reckoned Mickey was more than capable of selling the whole lot for five bob in some second-hand shop.

"You go home at dinner-time, don't you, Carter? Good. Then I'll expect you to bring them with you this afternoon. Now see you don't forget."

"No, sir."

When Joe intercepted the boy coming into school at the end of the lunch-hour, it seemed his worst fears had been partially realized. Mickey had the two general books with him, but the other, *Averingerett, Four Centuries of Growth*, a lavishly illustrated and expensively produced volume, was missing.

"But where is it?" he demanded, putting on (without much difficulty) his we-have-ways-of-making-you-talk voice.

"Don't know," said Mickey miserably. "I must 'ave lost it."

"But where boy, *where*?" asked Joe. "Where did you take the books?"

"Home."

"Then it must be at home. Or did you lose it on the way home?"

"Don't know, sir."

"But when did you notice it was missing?"

"Don't know, sir."

Joe groaned in exasperation.

"Please, sir," said the boy. "My dad says if you'll tell him what it cost, he'll pay you for it."

"Too bloody true," said Joe viciously. "I'll write him a letter."

He went away, raging inwardly. But it was Friday afternoon and the nearness of the weekend worked its balm.

"It was my own fault," he was able to say to Maggie philosophically halfway through the afternoon. "I should have known better."

"No," she said seriously. "You did the right thing."

It was nice to be approved of, thought Joe, but these occasional evidences of something like a sense of vocation in Maggie sometimes bothered him. He felt their relationship was within hailing distance of becoming serious (perhaps he could persuade his mother that "Cohen" was really "Cowan" or better still, "Colquhoun?") but he wasn't certain that Maggie really understood his character.

"Maggie," he said. "You must realize now, I am

*what I seem to be. When I propose intercourse in the
English store-cupboard between periods, I mean it.
And as for my work here, you've got to understand
that beneath my surface frivolity lie unplumbed depths
of unbelievable irresponsibilty."*

Even then she'd probably think he was joking.
How much of a shock would the revelation of the
real Joe Askern be to her?

But such sombre thoughts had vanished from
his mind as he clattered up the stairs to his flat,
pausing only to help himself to Alice's evening
paper which she must have forgotten to cancel
and which it seemed a shame to waste.

He quickly read through the few letters that had
arrived for him. His mother described another vic-
torious encounter she had had with the local hous-
ing office, before going on to wonder once more
whether he had yet found a "nice" girl.

All the time, bemoaned Joe. They're all nice, too
bloody nice.

He put the letter aside, poured himself a large
glass of milk and settled down to read Alice's local
paper.

Averingerett it seemed was local enough to rate
front-page attention here. The reporter had tried
to make something of it, but there wasn't a great
deal. The headline was GUIDE-BOOK BURGLARS
FOILED and beneath there was a picture of Jock
Laidlaw, the head steward, looking seriously into
the camera. Joe was glad to see it as it meant his
friend must have recovered. He was quoted as
saying the would-be burglars had not had a chance.
They hadn't even penetrated the first line of defences, having set off an alarm while trying to
force a ground-floor window in the north wing, which
in any case would only have let them into the

former chief groom's room which was quite cut off from every part of the building but the old stables.

Joe was amused, but the explanation of the headline caused the smile to fade slowly from his face.

Beneath the window the burglars had tried to force, and almost certainly dropped by them in their anxiety to escape, had been found a book. It was L. E. Othurst's *Averingerett, Four Centuries of Growth.* The journalist essayed some rather heavy-handed humour on the subject of noble lords throwing open their houses to the general public, but Joe was in no mood to appreciate it. The dreadful suspicion had leapt ready formed into his mind that the book was his.

Cess Carter! Eager for Mickey to go on the trip. To "case" the place? Why not, if as he suspected the boy had already served a fairly successful apprenticeship in breaking-and-entering? Then to borrow the books! Check what was most worth taking. Have a look at the diagrams of the layout of the building. Not that that seemed to have done them much good! But the bloody, infuriating cheek of the man!

Joe's instinct was always to avoid trouble. And Cess Carter frightened him. But sometimes in sheer reaction against his own awareness of this inclination to discretion, he would rush into a course of action quite uncharacteristic.

Like now.

Grabbing his jacket he rushed from the flat and sent his Volkswagen roaring up the road like a Panzer division. His intention was simple—to have words with Cess Carter.

"Listen Carter, you've gone too far this time. Don't deny it, you ginger thug, or I'll beat the yellow guts out of you. We're going to have a talk with Sergeant Prince, you and me. And you're going to be going

*away for a little holiday and perhaps while you're
away Mrs. Carter and me can try to make something
of that boy of yours, something you won't recognize."*

It was interesting to observe Maggie's educational influence already at work. So much for honesty.

The interview that took place was slightly different.

Firstly, by the time he found the Carters' house the initial outburst of indignation had shrunk to a dribble. The house itself was a surprise. For some reason he had decided on a corporation "semi"; instead he found himself outside a fairly imposing old terraced house, fallen somewhat from its original late-Victorian dignity perhaps, but solid, imposing still, and no shabbier than the town-hall, say, or the municipal baths. Skivvies had obviously skivvied here and perhaps even butlers buttled. It gave him pause.

Secondly, it was Mrs. Carter who answered his rap with the lion's-head knocker. She was wearing an apron and had obviously just come from the kitchen. There was flour on one of her hands and a trace of it was transferred to her forehead as she brushed back a lock of hair which had strayed forward. Her eyes widened with surprise, then worry, at the sight of Joe.

"Mr. Askern!" she said. "Why . . . there's nothing happened to Michael, is there?"

"No, no," he hurriedly reassured her, at the same time wondering why the boy hadn't got back from school yet. "I just wanted to have a word with your husband if I could. Is he in?"

"Yes, I think so. Come in, here's me keeping you on doorstep." Her anxiety was obviously not yet quite assuaged. "Is it about Michael you want to see him?"

Joe decided on part of the truth.

"Yes, that's right, Mrs. Carter. It's about a book I lent the boy. There were three actually, but he seems to have mislaid one. He probably mentioned it to you."

"Books?" she said, puzzled (understandably perhaps) by the thought of Mickey and books being linked together. "No, he said nowt to me. I didn't know he'd borrowed them even."

Joe's suspicions hardened. Obviously the whole arrangement had been a private one between Mickey and his father.

"Perhaps if I could just see Mr. Carter," he said gently.

"Aye," she said. "I'll give him a shout."

She ushered him into what had been, and probably still was known as, the front parlour. He watched her go out, noting the worried lines on her brow, the slight bend of her well-built shoulders. She must have been a good-looking woman in her youth. She couldn't be all that old now, forty-two, forty-three. But a life with Cess, and then fifteen years of Mickey (Joe was quite happy to believe in the boy's instant criminality), had obviously left its mark.

He began to feel guilty. He had no desire to make things worse for the poor woman. Also the springs of his indignation had been quite dried up by his encounter with her, and the menacing image of Carter began to loom large in his mind. Discretion as well as decency advised withdrawal. Perhaps Cess was out? He was certainly taking a long time to come.

Gently he opened the door and stepped into the hallway. His hopes of escape were dashed by the sound of upraised voices, one clearly Cess's, coming from the room opposite.

"You've been at it again, haven't you?" cried Mrs. Carter, outraged. "The minute I take my eyes off you. First the school, now this. I knew it, I knew it as soon as I read about it."

"It's all right, Mother," said Cess placatingly. "Nothing to worry about. It's all fixed. There'll be no bother."

"No bother! You're nothing but bother. There were conditions when I took you back, Cess. I warned you. Once more, I said. Just once more . . ."

"It's all right," repeated Cess. "I'll fix it. There'll be no bother. It won't happen again, believe me."

If she'll believe that, she'll believe anything, thought Joe, his indignation reviving. He'll fix it, will he? She'd be better off with him back in jail!

He rapped on the door and flung it open. They turned to look at him, Cess looking conciliatory, his wife's face set with anger.

When they saw who it was, their expressions slowly changed faces.

"Mr. Askern, I'm sorry . . . I didn't mean to keep you waiting . . ." began Mrs. Carter.

"What the hell are you up to, barging in like this?" demanded Cess furiously. "I was right about you first time. You're a snooper!"

Joe ignored him.

"It's all right, Mrs. Carter. I haven't come to make bother. Don't get upset."

His sympathetic tone was too much for the woman. Tears started to her eyes.

"Please don't upset yourself," repeated Joe.

"I try not to," she said, choking back a sob. "But it can be hard. I'll just go and sit down, if you don't mind. I'll be all right. I'll give my sister a ring, it'll be good to talk with someone who understands. If I'd taken her advice, I'd never be in this bother. Thanks, Mr. Askern."

With one last condemnatory glance at Cess, she went through the door which Joe held open for her.

"You're a swine, Carter," he said, feeling very noble. "She's a good woman. You can't go on treating her like dirt. She took you back when many another would have left you for good. Can't you see how lucky you are, man?"

Traditionally such a speech should have had strong men weeping in their beer. But Cess seemed remarkably unaffected.

"You think so, Sir?" he said with a sneer. "What's it to you?"

"It's a lot to me," said Joe indignantly. "I know what you've been up to. That's my bloody book they found at Averingerett, isn't it? And you put your lad up to borrowing it. God, how low can you get, involving an innocent boy in all this?"

That didn't ring very true even to Joe's ears. Mickey and innocence had long been strangers, he felt.

"I don't understand what you're saying," said Cess. "I don't think anyone else would either."

"Oh, wouldn't they? You think I'll keep quiet because I'm sorry for Mrs. Carter, don't you? Well, we'll have to see about that."

Turning on his heel Joe strode out of the door and down the hallway. Mrs. Carter looked up in alarm from the telephone as he marched past. He gave her a reassuring nod and opened the front door.

The evening sunshine fell across him like a hero's robe. It had really happened! He had been strong, stern, unbending. He had stood up to the bully. And he had survived.

If only he could re-phrase his parting words.

They could have been a little nobler, he felt. Still, they had been spoken, that was the main thing.

Exulting, he opened the door of the VW.

He was halfway into the driving-seat before he realized the car was not empty.

Lord Jim was squatting toad-like on the back seat. He acknowledged Joe's presence with a nod like a sledge-hammer.

Joe tried to get out again but a flat, spade-like hand rested on his arm, restraining him without effort.

"Well, Joe," said Carter's voice from the pavement. "Mind if I join you two? Let's go somewhere and have a drink and see if we can't clear up this little misunderstanding."

CHAPTER V

"No" said Joe. "I don't want another drink."

Without doing something absurdly dramatic like crashing the car, or screaming out for help, it had been difficult not to go with Carter and Lord Jim. It was daylight, the pub they had taken him to appeared fairly respectable. The few drinkers already present so early in the evening looked as if they had just dropped in for a quick one on their way home from work. It was difficult to feel menaced.

But he kept a firm grip on the glass in front of him and refused to let it be replenished, even though the conversation was making another double more and more desirable.

"Cards on the table, Joe," said Carter. "You were right. It was your book. And it *was* Lord Jim and me at Averingerett last night. We left in a bit of a hurry. Good job your book didn't have your name in, eh?"

He grinned broadly.

"Why are you telling me this?" asked Joe, realizing that while false suspicions just make a man look foolish, confirmed suspicions can terrify.

"We need your help, Joe," said Carter earnestly, bringing his face close to Joe's. "That's why we're telling you. No, wait a minute, listen. What you've got to understand is that Jim here and me, we're in the business. Right? We're thieves. Professionals."

Lord Jim nodded. Whenever he did this, Joe had

the feeling it was not just acquiescence but a rehearsal for a deathblow.

"Professionals!" he tried to sneer. "There wasn't very much professional about last night."

Carter looked sheepish.

"No. Well, all we really went for was a look around. Just a probe. Just to confirm what we had known all along."

"What's that?."

"That to get into the place and out again without attracting notice, we need you."

"Me! You must be—I'm leaving!"

Jim's hand on his knee changed his mind.

"You see, Joe, it's always been a dream of mine to do a place like this," said Cess. "All that loot, all sitting there, asking for it. But it's not like popping down the road one night, ringing up Mr. Money's house to make sure he's out, then forcing the kitchen window. No, a job like this needs expert planning. And it needs contacts."

He leaned on his elbows, nodding in agreement with himself.

"That's you, Joe. On both counts. You came along like a gift from heaven. You might say you gave us the idea, so you're in on it already."

"Not me," said Joe. "You can't involve me, Carter."

The enormity of what the man was saying continued to dawn on him.

"You rotten bastard! So you sent your son along to look over the place and to borrow my books! You must be mad!"

"Not to look over the place," corrected Cess. "To look over *you*. We were impressed by what he told us. Knows the place like the back of his hand does Jojo (that's what they call you, I told him to watch his lip!), and what's more, he's in with all the stewards, takes his sandwiches along to the head steward's room."

"Why, the young yobbo! Spying on me!" said Joe indignantly.

"Hush," said Cess reprovingly. "He's a good lad. He can do you favours. I've told him to see you have a nice easy ride in that school. No pins on Sir's seat, or scratches on his little kraut car. Haven't you noticed?"

Oh no, groaned Joe internally. I'm being protected by a fifteen-year-old delinquent!

Out loud he tried to speak with calmness and conviction. There seemed to be two courses open. One was to agree and then go and tell the police as soon as possible. The other was to refuse, but pledge silence. To refuse *and* tell the police needed more courage than he had available at the moment.

"Look," he said, "I can't help you. I don't want to, and even if I did, I know nothing about the place you can't pick up yourself by reading a couple of guide-books. So you stick to your business, I'll stick to mine. I'll forget all about this conversation . . ."

"Will you?" said Cess childishly. "Honest? No, I doubt it, lad. Somehow I doubt it."

"Why not?" said Joe eagerly. "Look, who'd believe me? And you haven't done anything. Yet. I kept quiet about the clock . . . and . . ."

"I was right about you, Joe," said Cess with satisfaction. "You've got a head on your shoulders. Drunk, and you still noticed that stuff. And had enough sense to say nowt. You're one of us already, you know that?"

"Hello Cess, hello Jim. Thought I'd find you here. Who's getting me a drink?"

It was Cynthia, tightly-sweatered, minimally-skirted, her heavy, red lips curved in a smile of greeting which faded as Carter hooked back with his foot the chair she was pulling out from under the table.

"We're busy, Cyn," he said coldly. "Shove off."

"What? Busy? Sitting here having a drink, that's busy? I'd like to be kept busy like that!" she answered indignantly.

Cess half-rose.

"Shove off, girl, when you're told, and stop the gabber, or I'll break your bloody jaw and stop it for you."

Cynthia visibly paled, opened her mouth as if to answer back, changed her mind and flounced off to the far end of the bar.

She had the buttocks for a magnificent flounce, Joe was able to note before his previous emotions reasserted themselves.

"All right, Joe," said Carter, any suspicion of a conciliatory, friendly note gone from his voice. "I've offered you a job, a chance to make a bit of spare cash. Purely in an advisory capacity. What's your answer?"

"Answer? I'm not—how can—I don't know," said Joe helplessly. Answer? How can a man answer a question like that with a thug like Lord Jim holding his leg and a face like Carter's two inches in front of him?

"He wants time to think, I expect, Jim," said Carter finally. "We'll give him time. Tonight. Let him sleep on it. We'll see him in the morning. But remember, Joe, Lord Jim here is the youngest of seven and they'll all be watching you. So just think on, don't talk, eh? And make up your mind right. Otherwise I wouldn't bother to waste time marking any homework this evening."

He stood up and left, followed closely by Jim.

Cynthia turned on her bar stool as they passed but they ignored her and disappeared through the door.

"Carter!" Joe yelled after them. "Your breath smells, you know that? I've had time to think and the answer's no. So go home and start packing, lad. And tell Quasimodo there to go and climb a bell-rope. If he comes near me again I'll tread on him so hard, he'll be able to reminisce arterwards about when he was big."

"Scotch. A double," Joe said. His weak legs had carried him to the bar in response to the urgent message his brain had been pumping out for the past ten minutes.

"What about serving me first?" demanded Cynthia angrily. "These bloody men think they own the earth."

The barman paused, undecided. Joe waved his hand.

"Serve the lady, please. I'm sorry if I jumped the queue."

"That's all right, love," said Cyn, somewhat mollified. She came down the bar towards him. "Here, it's Sir, isn't it? From the Bell?"

"The name's Joe," said Joe.

"That's right," she said. "I put you to bed. Took your trousers off. You're all right," she added enigmatically.

"Well thanks," said Joe. "Here let me pay for that."

"If you like," the woman said indifferently. "Oh that bastard! I'd like to . . ."

"Carter?" said Joe, relieved to talk rather than think, even if it was about the cause of his troubles.

She looked at him sharply.

"You two friends? I thought you was a teacher or something?"

"No. I don't think we're friends."

"Oh. That's all right then. He can be nasty . . ."
Joe drank most of his scotch with a shudder.

"Did you see the way he treated me. I've a good mind to . . ."

"What?"

"I don't know," she said hopelessly.

"Have another drink," he said, finishing his.

"I'll pay for these," she said and when he protested, went on, "Look, love, you're not picking me up or something, I'll stand my round."

They took their drinks to a corner table.

"How long have you known Carter?" asked Joe with some notion of getting better acquainted with his enemy.

"Too bloody long," she said gloomily. "Why're you interested?"

"Just making conversation."

"Well, make it about something else. And take a tip from me. Don't get mixed up with Cess if you can help it. You're not the type."

"Believe me, I won't," he said fervently.

His initial impression of Cynthia as a stupid sex-kitten in the Hollywood "gangster's moll" tradition proved to be unfounded. She talked readily and entertainingly in a rather earthy fashion of herself and her upbringing, always stopping short of her involvement with Carter. She described herself as a professional escort working for an "agency," which she indignantly insisted was legitimate when Joe permitted himself a knowing smile. It was up to her, she protested. She only went as far as personal inclination took her.

"Well, usually," she added with gloomy honesty.

They both bought another round and Joe's mind was beginning to be able to face the future without the chilling sweat breaking out under his armpits.

What after all can he do? he thought confidently.
I might even pop along and have a word with
Sergeant Prince.

He glanced at his watch to see if it was good
popping-along time. It was twenty-five past seven.

"Jesus!" he said. "Maggie!"

He rose a little unsteadily to his feet.

"Are you going?" said Cynthia, making a moue
of disappointment. "I was just enjoying our chat."

Flattered, Joe waved his arms in regret. The
image of Maggie was very blurred in his mind and
the living physical (very physical) presence of Cynthia had very real attractions. But of course an
arrangement had been made, Maggie would be
ready and waiting, it was impossible to make other
plans now.

Cynthia took his arm and pulled him down
towards her so that she could speak in his ear. His
forearm was pressed within the deep canyon between her breasts.

"I thought we'd probably end up by going back
to your place," she whispered, "and . . ."

Flabbergasted, he sat down, one part of his mind
completely incredulous of the graphically expressed
suggestion she had just made, but another part
sending urgent messages to the extremes of his
body. She leaned across the table and even more
incredibly he felt her hand come between his legs.

"There," she said with a smile. "I told you I
could see you were all right."

Without the drink, Joe told himself, without the
drink, this would not be possible. I wouldn't sit
here and listen to such talk, and allow myself to be
. . . caressed. I'd get up, and go, and Maggie will
be waiting and . . . Without the drink . . .

"Let's have another drink," he said hoarsely.

"One," she said. "One for the road."

It sounded the most depraved thing ever said in the history of the world.

Half an hour later they came out of the pub together closely entwined. Joe did not know whether he was going to be able to hold out till they got home. He didn't protest when she took the car key from him and climbed in the driving-seat. It left both his hands free for the assault. Suddenly he remembered his first sighting of Cess and Cyn in the old Consul stuck at the traffic lights. The memory sent him into fits of laughter, and Cynthia was able to get the car moving.

The stairs up to his flat presented him with another opportunity for falling against her and indulging in tight, exploratory embraces.

"Christ," she said. "You're impetuous."

"It's all right," he said, unzipping her skirt. "The house is empty. I know. Let's do it on the stairs."

"I'm too old for that," she said. "I like my comforts."

Once inside the flat, there was no more resistance, just a session of hilarious confusion as they undressed each other. Either from longer practice or greater sobriety she was the more efficient and he found himself stark naked while Cynthia still had a couple of flimsy bits of silk to go.

"Hang on a sec, love," she said, side-stepping his desperate lunge with ease. She burrowed into her handbag and came up with a cigarette case.

"Here," she said, offering it to him. "Try one."

"Christ," he said. "Not now! Later. First things . . ."

He lunged and missed again. She caught his arm and held it tight in some kind of wrestler's lock.

"Silly," she said. "What do you think I am? They're not bloody Players. Try one. They'll make it even better."

The way he felt at the moment, Joe was unable to envisage any improvement on what he proposed. But he let Cyn slip the thin tube of paper between his lips and set a match to it while he awkwardly removed the rest of her clothes.

"Now puff," she said. "That's it. Nice and deep. Puff. Puff. There now. There now. Isn't that better?"

Joe wasn't sure. It was certainly different. There seemed to have been a shift in the dimensions of the familiar room and Cynthia herself seemed blurred and distant. At the same time he felt himself possessed of a strangely heightened sensitivity to sense impressions and there seemed to have been a shift in his own personal dimensions to make him even better equipped to deal with the matter in hand.

He approached Cynthia to put this to the test. She seemed eager to co-operate; his sense of touch at least found nothing blurred or distant about her, though their activities seemed to be taking place in a kind of eggshell-blue cocoon, as though they were locked together in a slice of early summer sky.

"Through here, through here," whispered Cynthia, leading him to where only a very old memory told him the bedroom was.

Normally any sense of removal from reality was extremely painful to Joe. He enjoyed getting drunk, but the actuality of being drunk, with all its unsteadiness and dizziness, was a terrible nightmare to him. Now however his present lack of orientation meant nothing to him. Every locomotory need was being very well taken care of by Cynthia, who seemed to have developed about fifteen hands, and his sense of suspension in time and space only served to intensify the delightful things which were happening to him. It was true that from time to time the sky-blue cocoon seemed to explode in a burst of white light. And once or twice memories that Cyn was Cess's girl swam to the surface of his consciousness and he seemed to hear the man's voice muttering menacingly in his ear. But these illusions were as nothing compared with the joy of finding extraordinary portions of himself coming into contact with extraordinary portions of Cynthia. And even when for a moment her face swam into sudden perfect focus before his eyes and his fevered imagination painted a shiny black moustache on the upper lip, even then he was amused rather than distressed and chuckled to himself as he resumed the delightful task of imprinting his initials in love-bites along her left buttock. How he had managed to see her face at all from this position was a problem he postponed for future consideration.

Finally either from exhaustion, or the effects of drink, or perhaps of the cigarette (definitely not Players), the blue cocoon darkened and contracted, finally crushing him in blackness.

When he awoke, he was alone, neatly tucked up in bed. So neatly in fact that it was with difficulty that he managed to push the sheet and single blanket down from his chest and sit up.

The room was clean and tidy, showing no signs whatever of the wild activity he dimly remembered. Indeed the memory was so dim that he began to wonder if it had not all happened in his mind, but his own physical fragility and a strong sense of general euphoria whenever he tried to pierce the mists convinced him that a great deal must have really happened.

No wonder Coleridge couldn't manage all of *Kubla Khan*, he thought.

The doorbell rang.

"A person from Porlock," he said, pulling his dressing-gown over his naked shoulders.

But when he opened the door the person from Porlock turned out to be two persons, unwelcome no matter from where they came.

Cess and Lord Jim.

He slammed the door shut with a force that would have crushed anyone else's foot, but Lord Jim's face remained a blank as he effortlessly pushed the door back with his left hand.

"Morning, Joe," said Carter stepping into the room, a jovial smile arcing unconvincingly over his cunning animal face. "Time's up."

"No," said Joe. "I mean, no. Look, I have to *think*."

"You've had all night," said Carter mildly.

"Yes. No. I was . . . busy. I didn't have time."

What the hell time *is* it? he wondered. Carter answered him by drawing the curtains and letting in strong shafts of late morning sunlight.

"Not have time?" he echoed. "Don't tell me you were busy all night, eh? Not just the drink then with you, eh Joe? By God, you're a right dark horse. What do you say, Jim?"

Lord Jim said nothing.

"Anyone we know?" asked Carter.

Does he know? *He knows*! How *can* he know? Please God, don't *let* him know, prayed Joe.

"No," he said.

"No?" said Carter. "Someone from school, perhaps? The domestic science lass, Miss Coon or something? My lad says he reckons you fancy your chances there."

"No, no," said Joe, remembering for the first time since seven-twenty-five the previous evening that he had had a date with Maggie.

Sickness, he thought. A sudden bereavement. A slight car accident, perhaps?

His need to start constructing excuses despite his present predicament made him wonder just how serious he was getting about the girl. Not all that serious if you considered the speed with which she dropped completely out of his mind at Carter's next words.

"Someone else at school then? Oh, Joe, Joe boy," he said in avuncularly reproving tones, "you've not been after any of those young lasses, have you? Not that Maisie Uppadine for instance?"

Oh the bastard! that young bastard Mickey! He must have noticed the effect Maisie's magnificent breasts had on him and reported home. Was it so obvious then? God, he'd fix him, he'd fix him good!

"Certainly not," he said coldly. "What an absurd suggestion."

"Ay, probably so," said Carter. "Probably so. Only, I thought after seeing *this*; well, it does make you wonder."

This which he handed to Joe now, sent his mind reeling into a state reminiscent of the night before. It was a photostat copy of the Maisie-poem.

"How . . . ?" he asked, "how . . . what . . . this is absurd! Absurd!"

"True," said Carter. "Very true. I *know* you, Joe. You wouldn't do a thing like that. Not with the girl only *fifteen*. You're an honest, above-board kind of fellow, Joe. That's why I want you to work with us. What about it, Joe?"

Joe's mind raced. The implied threat was obvious. Help these two with their half-baked wholly criminal schemes, or the poem would be used. How had they got it? Cynthia, the bitch! Which meant that Carter *must* know! Which meant . . . but no time now to follow up that line of thought. No, these goons thought they were being clever, but what they didn't realize was that the straight-forward threat of physical violence was potentially more frightening to him than anything they could do with the poem. His writing was not particularly distinctive; at worst they could put him in a position where he would have to lie, evade, embroider, be indignant; whereas lost teeth, broken ribs and whatever unthinkable damage might result from Lord Jim's boot in his groin were the kind of things his peculiar talents were not suited to avoid.

"This is outrageous," he said. "I've never seen this *filth* before."

He screwed up the paper and threw it at the fireplace where it bounced from the gas-fire on to the carpet.

"Nor have I any intention of helping you pursue any of your criminal ventures. Good day."

He liked the sound of that. And he had actually said it out loud, something he rarely did with his best utterances. He felt a glow of pleasure as he strode to the door and flung it open.

"Go now," he said.

The two men looked at him expressionlessly but made no move.

"Please," he added.

"Now, Joe," said Carter, "we're not trying to force your hand. We know no one in their right senses would believe anything bad of you just on the strength of something like this."

He produced another copy of the poem. He seemed to have a thick wad of them in his inside pocket.

"However," he said, "if people were to see things like *these*, they might begin to wonder. Show him, Jim."

These, which Lord Jim handed over, were a couple of dozen postcard-sized photographs. Joe looked at the top one and closed the door violently. Unbelieving, he thumbed quickly through the rest. Carter had come up behind him and was looking with interest over his shoulder.

"That's my favourite," he said stopping Joe's incredulous shuffle. "That's what I call ingenious."

The photos without exception showed Joe himself, stark naked, in a series of complex sexual negotiations with a woman obviously Cynthia, though her full face never appeared. The one Carter so admired brought to mind Maggie's query whether anyone ever *did* hang naked from a chandelier. There was no chandelier in the flat, but the principle involved was clearly demonstrated.

"But you should really see the ciné-film," said Carter. "Now that is really something, isn't it, Jim?"

"I don't understand," said Joe piteously, but already he was beginning to recall the flashes of white light which from time to time had seemed to penetrate his delirium the night before, and the sound of Carter's voice, and something else besides . . .

"What we thought we'd do," said Carter, "is spread these round a bit. A friend of ours has a little business, lots of outlets, we're looking after them for the moment while he sorts out a spot of bother . . ."

"Chubb!" said Joe, putting a name to the black-moustached face which had hovered over him momentarily. Lining up a shot. Oh my God!

"You know him?" asked Carter. "That's nice. Yes, little Tommy. He's always ready to do a friend a favour and me, I've been a real friend to him, haven't I, Jim? Well, he'll have to tread carefully, of course, until things get sorted out, but he's got a lot of pull. Meanwhile, I'm in charge and I say . . ."

This was different. No amount of explanation, prevarication, or indignation, could stop people seeing that the man in the photographs was Joe Askern, schoolteacher, and there weren't any words to lessen their effect.

I was drunk, sounded bad. *I was drugged*, worse. *I didn't realize I was being photographed* was just absurd. In any case Chubb had been so expert that frequently it seemed as if Joe was smiling with modest self-congratulation right into the camera.

"You know," said Carter, pressing home his advantage, "the case against Tommy is getting under way. We could even arrange for some of these to come into the hands of the police as evidence."

He brought this out as though it were a clincher. He and Lord Jim stared appraisingly at Joe as if expecting him to collapse completely under the threat.

His actual reaction completely surprised them and for the first time since their arrival they were not in full command of the situation.

Joe spread out the pictures on the floor and knelt over them, his shoulders jerking. A sound like a sob came from his mouth, was repeated, and again, increasing in volume. Cess stepped forward, worried, but now Joe flung back his head and let peal after peal of laughter come pouring out till the tears started up in his eyes.

"What's so bloody funny?" asked Lord Jim, speaking for the first time. He moved forward menacingly.

"You wouldn't understand," said Joe, still laughing, but something in Jim's demeanour made him attempt an explanation. "It's Miss Onions. I was thinking of Miss Onions in the jury-box suddenly been asked to examine *these*."

Once more he rocked forward on his knees and laughed long and loud. Carter smiled too. He could detect the desperate note of hysteria in the laughter now.

CHAPTER VI

Joe's first reaction after Carter and Lord Jim had gone was to be sick. Fear may have helped, but he was realistic enough to acknowledge the strong alcoholic stimulus from the previous evening.

After that, feeling surprisingly better, he dressed, went out and bought a copy of *The Times Educational Supplement.*

There seemed to be very little staff turnover in the West Country. The choice seemed to lie between being housemistress in a residential comprehensive school in Cornwall and a peripatetic violin teacher in South Devon.

He had a momentarily pleasing picture of himself strolling along leafy lanes, fiddling gaily, with a charivari of happy children in his wake. It was a pity he couldn't play. Now, if it had been a peripatetic ocarinist . . .

Perhaps he had better be content with something not quite so distant.

But it was all foolishness in any case, he thought, tossing the paper to one side. It wasn't a question of distance, it was a question of time. Cess might be a big-shot locally, but he obviously wasn't the king-pin of an international or even national criminal organization. Move thirty miles north to Leeds and he'd probably be safe. On second thoughts make that west to Manchester. He'd be happier over the Penines. And he doubted if Cess would risk the police interest his own counter-accusations would cause should he go ahead and publish the pictures out of spite.

So why worry?

Because I can't move from here till the end of term, even supposing I get another job, he answered himself. Not if I want to go on being a teacher, and what else am I fit for? And if I *do* stay on here and *don't* go along with Cess, Lord Jim'll be paying me a visit. And those photos may start circulating. Oh, Onions, Onions! How will you triumph! How arrogantly will you parade your justified instincts about me! Have I the right to inflict *that* on my dear colleagues? Me, with my broken arms, cracked ribs and missing teeth?

The intrusion into his thoughts, even rhetorically, of his colleagues suddenly brought Maggie back to his mind. Maggie who must have sat in growing concern all the previous evening waiting for him to arrive.

He picked up the phone and dialled her number. Her mother answered. He had never met Mrs. Cohen and the mental image created by her voice when he announced his name made him anxious to postpone an encounter. Maggie wasn't there, said Mrs. Cohen. Maggie wouldn't be there all day. Nor tomorrow either.

"Well, I'll see her at school on Monday," said Joe hopelessly. "Tell her . . ."

But he was talking to the dialling tone which sounded, on the whole, rather friendlier than Maggie's mother.

What the hell, thought Joe gloomily. I'm in no condition to face a round of explanation and recrimination now. I'll think up something by Monday.

Momentarily the thought did flash across his still foggy mind like a gleam of breast behind a fan-dancer's feathers that the only sensible thing to do was pick up the phone again and ring Sergeant Prince. But it seemed easier to sit down for a few minutes and let his fears drown beneath the liquid notes of Garland singing "Look for the Silver Lining." Vardon, who had dematerialized as soon as Lord Jim had knocked at the door, now reappeared and added his comfort by purring loudly out of time with the music.

Later he felt sufficiently recovered to venture out in search of something to eat. Despite his growing optimism that some solution to his problems would turn up, he found himself acting like a man on the run, looking up and down the street half a dozen times before stepping out from behind the front door, and glancing frequently into his driving-mirror as he drove into the shopping centre.

After a light meal, which was all his stomach was still fit for, he did his weekend shopping and afterwards went to the early performance at the local cinema. He wasn't particularly interested in the picture, but he had no other plans, having half-assumed he would be seeing something more of Maggie over the weekend.

He left before the end of the film, drawing a disapproving cluck from an old dear next to him.

"Paul Newman's a double agent," he whispered confidentially, and felt immediately ashamed.

I'm a big man when it comes to putting down old women, he thought. But Cess and Lord Jim have just got to look at me to make me sweat.

Damn them both! he thought angrily as he spiralled down from the multi-storey car-park. Why should I let a couple of small-time crooks bother me?

I'll put on the pressure for a change, he told himself as he drove home through the empty streets of the early evening. I've got at least as much to threaten them with as they have me. *I've* broken no law, *I* can't be sent to gaol.

He slammed the garage door shut with a force which mirrored his new resolution and strode manfully across the garage forecourt. The small block of rental garages contrasted oddly in style and material with the backs of the terraced houses in one of which his flat was situated. These terraces hadn't been built to look at from behind, he thought as he pushed open the rickety wooden door which led to the back yard and garden.

Still, it's home.

His arm was grasped at the elbow. With a certainty usually reserved only for lovers, he knew the touch.

"Cess wants a word," said Lord Jim.

Cess was standing against the yard wall manicuring his fingernails with a knife, like a man who has seen too many pre-war Warner Brothers gangster films.

"You've got a visitor, Joe," he said flatly.

"Oh?" Absurdly his mind began to tick off the friends and relatives who might possibly visit him.

"Don't you want to know who? Or perhaps he does know who already. What do you think, Jim?"

Jim was invisible behind him, but Joe felt his presence, dark and menacing.

"Jim's not sure. Which is lucky for you. If Jim was sure, I wouldn't know any way to stop him marking you."

It suddenly seemed the best idea in the world to stop Jim from becoming sure.

"Who?" asked Joe drily. "Who is it?"

Cess didn't answer immediately but studied his fingernails speculatively. The knife looked old and stained.

"Prince," he said finally. "Sergeant bloody Prince. What's he want, Joe?"

"How the hell should I know?"

Suddenly they were both very close, not speaking, not touching, but unbearably, threateningly close. He could not see the knife but his feverish imagination placed it an inch away from his rib-cage.

"I don't know," he cried. "I hardly know the man. Perhaps he's worried about the company I keep!"

Fear had made him unintentionally ironic, but it seemed to break the tension. Cess stepped back, smiling. The knife had disappeared.

"You could be right, Joe. You probably are. As long as you didn't send for him, eh? But I can see you didn't. I told you we could rely on him, Jim! But you'll be careful, won't you? Be like a good citizen. Only remember, the only good citizen is a live citizen."

"We'll be around," growled Lord Jim.

"That's right. So watch how you go, Joe."

Silently they slid out through the wooden door. Joe waited a good five minutes in the yard before he felt able to go into the house.

Perhaps, he thought hopefully, Prince will have tired of waiting and gone away.

At first he thought his hope had been realized. There was no sign of the sergeant either in the hall or on the first-floor landing. But his sigh of relief was interrupted by the opening of a door below and Alice's voice.

"That you, Joe?"

"Yes."

"Visitor."

"Thank you very much, Miss-er-Fletcher. Very

kind of you. Good night." It was Prince's voice. Followed by Prince's tread up the stairs.

"Mr. Askern? Can you spare a moment?"

"Of course," said Jim. "Come in."

Prince refused a drink saying he had just had a coffee with Alice in her flat. He stressed the word *coffee.*

"Very hospitable neighbour you have," he said. "Very *generous* girl. If she hadn't asked me in, I'd have probably gone away and missed you."

Damn the woman! groaned Joe inwardly. Why did she have to be so desperate for men?

"What can I do for you, Sergeant?" he asked.

"Have you known Cess Carter long?" said Prince.

Hot and cold waves ran the length of Joe's body so violently that he felt their progress must be clearly visible.

"Carter?" he croaked. "Oh, you mean Mickey's father?"

"That's right. You were playing golf with him last Sunday."

"No. No. Not really. I mean yes, I was playing with him, but we just happened to meet. That's all. I met him for the first time at a PTA meeting a few days before. I teach his son."

"I'd like to think so," said Prince with a smile.

"Why do you ask?" said Joe.

"What do you know about Carter?" asked Prince, ignoring Joe's question.

"Nothing. Nothing much."

"Well, you must choose your own friends, Mr. Askern. But a man in your position has got to be circumspect. Carter's got a criminal record, you know that?"

"Yes, well. I had heard something."

"He's a professional criminal, Mr. Askern. A violent man. He's kept his nose clean for two or three years now, ever since his wife took him back."

"You mean, she left him?"

"That's right. Last time he got sent down. Just a couple of years. Small stuff, he stole half a church roof. Anyway his wife told him she'd had enough. I was there. I nicked him. She said if he was going to be a bloody fool all his life, at least he wasn't going to involve her and her son any more. True enough, when he came out, the door was locked in his face. She kept it up for six months, then she gave him another chance. It seemed to work for a while, but we've started hearing things lately. So we're keeping an eye on Cess and his associates, just in case they get any ideas above their station. Just routine."

Routine like hell! thought Joe. That's what they always say till they can send you down.

"Am I an associate then?" he asked, trying for a lightly surprised tone.

"No. No, of course not," said Prince, suddenly conciliatory. "It was just that seeing you together last Sunday, I got to wondering if he'd said anything interesting . . . to us, I mean."

"I'm not a whatsitsname . . . nark. Not a nark!" protested Joe.

Prince looked puzzled.

"Of course not," he said. "But you'd tell the police if you knew a crime was being planned, wouldn't you?"

"Certainly. Certainly," said Joe in his good citizen voice.

"Well then. I'm sorry to have troubled you."

"Not at all," said Joe, feeling very relieved. It had hardly been worth Prince's while coming to see him just for this. Strangely the thought did not comfort him.

"By the way," said the sergeant at the door. "I was round at the school this morning. Checking the new locks they had fitted after the break-in."

"Really? Anything new on that?" asked Joe casually.

"We've got a couple of ideas. Is your car OK now, by the way?"

The question baffled him. He examined it so closely for concealed pitfalls that Prince had to cough gently to remind him of the need for an answer.

"I don't follow . . ." was the best he could manage.

"Broke down that night, didn't it? One of the beat men noticed it standing outside the Bell all night."

"Yes. That is, no. I had a couple of drinks and thought I'd better catch a bus. Safer."

"Very wise," said Prince. "It's best to be safe. I met one of your colleagues at school this morning. Cohen, is it? *Miss* Cohen? She's not married?"

What's he trying to do to me? groaned Joe.

"No," he said. "She's not married."

"Nice girl. *Very* nice girl. We've nothing like that down at the station. You're a lucky man!" Prince laughed. "Well, must be off. Thanks for talking with me, Mr. Askern. Good night!"

Joe watched him go down the stairs and listened till he heard the front door close. Then he raced to the window overlooking the street to ensure that Prince had really left the house. The unmistakable mop of white hair was being carried purposefully across the road. Parked almost opposite the house was a car, a blue Cortina, whose driver was visible behind the wheel, reading a newspaper. Prince went by without the slightest pause in his stride, but Joe's gaze stayed on the car. He was sure he had seen it parked there once or twice recently. It made him feel uneasy. But this could just be an overflow from the great flood of unease released by Prince's visit. Could it just be coincidence that he had touched upon nearly every cause of concern in Joe's mind at the moment?

"Miaou!" said Vardon, rising from his eavesdropping position behind the record player.

It was time for food or Garland. Or both. Somewhere over the rainbow seemed a good place to be. But as he hacked open the tin of pilchards he and Vardon were going to share for supper, he had the feeling that it was already too late.

CHAPTER VII

"Nice weekend, Joe?"

The next bastard to ask me if I had a nice weekend gets a swift hack on the shin.

"Morning, Askern. Nice weekend?"

Except Solly. Headmasters should not be kicked except by winners of football pools.

In any case, no answer seemed to be required as Solstice went on, "I was out for a run in the car yesterday. Did you know there's a diversion on the A515 because of roadworks?"

"Did I know? No. Or yes, now you come to mention it, I think I did notice something on our Averingerett trip last weekend."

"I wondered about that," said Solly sadly, as though some awful suspicion had been confirmed. "You might have mentioned it, Askern."

He tottered off to his study to plant a red flag on his wall-map.

It must be marvellous, thought Joe, for your only worry to be keeping an up-to-date account of local road conditions.

"Morning, Joe," said Vernon coming into the staff-room with his Monday-morning Celtic twilight look. "Looked for you yesterday. I went round in a hundred and seven. I needed the sight of somebody worse."

"I stayed at home," said Joe. "A bit under the weather."

"Oh? Nothing serious?"

For a moment Joe thought of confiding his troubles to Vernon, but the sound of the assembly bell interrupted his thoughts. In any case, his woes required either a desert to shout them in, or a quiet corner and a confidential whisper.

As he made for the hall he caught a glimpse of Maggie's car pulling into the staff car-park. He increased his pace. He didn't feel able to meet her yet.

His story was fully prepared, of course. A visit to some friends in Sheffield, prior to calling on Maggie. A sudden attack of some unspecified illness—symptoms of nausea, fainting and so on. He wasn't too far from the truth. A visit from the doctor; unfit to drive; couldn't get through on the telephone, in any case semi-delirious.

It wasn't a great story, but it was fairly watertight and it established him away from the flat on Friday evening in case she'd tried to phone.

They met in the corridor as he returned from assembly. One look at her face told him things were going to be difficult. For the second time in twenty minutes, he thought of confessing all. But not here, not in a corridor with all the reluctant activity of an educational Monday morning about them.

He launched himself into his tale, looking for signs of softening as he described his illness. There were none. If anything the unwelcome signs flashed brighter. He sucked in his cheeks a little more, coughed gently, and essayed a little stagger. Still no effect. Quickly as he could, he got to the end of his story and paused.

She considered him for a moment, coldly and impersonally it seemed. It felt most unpleasant.

"So you were sick?"

"Yes."

"In Sheffield?"

"Yes."

"Where you spent the night?"

"Yes."

She smiled now, but grimly. If anything, he'd preferred the impersonal scrutiny.

"Then I think you should see the police."

Oh Jesus! What does she know?

"Because, being concerned when you didn't turn up and I couldn't get you on the phone, I drove round to your flat on Friday night."

Oh God. Such things shouldn't happen.

"I was just in time to see a man and a woman going in. I saw them quite clearly. They were moving slowly as there seemed to be some confusion whether or not they should keep their clothes on till they got inside."

No more. Please God, no more.

"Shortly afterwards your light went on. Obviously as you were in Sheffield, they were using your flat illegally. Don't you think you should report it?"

He spread his arms out in a hopeless gesture and avoided her eyes.

"I'm sorry, Maggie. Really sorry. I can explain . . ."

"Again? I heard you the first time, Joe. I won't bother with the repeat."

She pushed past him and strode away down the corridor.

"Maggie," he said turning after her. Mickey Carter stood a couple of yards away, grinning broadly.

"Morning, sir," he said. "How's it going?"

His head nearly came off as Joe caught him an open-handed round-armer behind the ear.

The rest of the day was black dark for Joe, relieved temporarily only by the news that Miss Onions had indeed been selected for service on the jury trying Chubb.

She'll put him away for ever! thought Joe gleefully, remembering the part the little pornographer's photography played in his present plight. But the rift in his relationship with Maggie had caused him too much pain for any lasting pleasure in anything. In fact, just as a broken leg takes one's mind off toothache, so the loss of Maggie almost made him forget Cess Carter and Lord Jim.

But only almost.

By four o'clock, things had changed insomuch as the processes of self-justification and self-pity had almost completed their cycles. And when Maggie ignored Joe's fifth attempt to speak to her as she went towards her car, he drove away furiously, picturing her painful remorse when, too late, she found out the truth. How nobly forgiving he would be!

Meanwhile he was resolved to go home and give Alice what she'd been begging for for months. If Maggie was going to nominate him lecherous bastard of the month, he might as well start acting the part.

Only the fact that Alice did not arrive home till five-thirty prevented him from putting his plan into immediate operation. At five twenty-five he was standing at his window looking along the street, eagerly awaiting her appearance.

At five-thirty the blue Cortina drove slowly past the house and came to a halt about twenty yards down the road. He felt extremely uneasy at the sight. Who the hell could it be?

But now his mind was diverted from the problem by the appearance of Alice, moving with easy grace, elegantly dressed, her slimness a definite asset in this area. He felt his blood begin to stir within him. Perhaps here he could finally shake off his obsession with big breasts. Could Alice be slotted into the Maisie poem? Who cared? He could always turn to a lesser poet to find the apt phrase for his present feelings.

"I begin to feel some rousing motions in me," he quoted softly, "Which dispose to something extraordinary my thoughts."

She looked up and saw him, waved hesitantly. He opened the window and leaned out. She stopped.

"Hello," she said. "How are you?"

"Much better," he said. "Care to share a poor bachelor's crust? I've got a huge pizza in the fridge just longing to be thrust into a red-hot oven for twenty minutes."

"Oh," she said, surprised at either his hospitality or his imagery. "That would be nice. Lovely. Yes, please. Now?"

"This very instant," he said. "Come as you are."

He withdrew from the window feeling very Caliph-ish and rubbed his hands as he glanced around the room, making sure all was in order.

Hurry up, love, he thought. For you, Christmas has come a little early this year.

He glanced at himself in the mirror and undid another button on his shirt.

There was a gentle tap at the door.

"Come in," he called. "It's open house."

Slowly the door swung open. Joe went towards it, a smile on his lips.

Lord Jim stepped solidly into the room.

"Oh no," said Joe.

"He wants to see you," said Jim.

"Not again. I can't come. Not now."

"Now," said Jim.

"It's early. It's only half past five."

"He's got other things to do later," said Jim.

"Hello!" said Alice from the doorway, her face faintly flushed, perhaps from running up the stairs. "Do you mind, I brought an apple pie and some cream."

She stopped as she caught sight of Lord Jim.

"Oh, sorry."

She smiled at him. Her smile died as he turned his slatey eyes on her and slowly looked her up and down.

"We'd better be off," he said.

Alice tore her fascinated gaze from him and looked in surprise at Joe. It seemed to be her look-of-the-night.

"I'm sorry," he said. It wasn't worth even a token protest he thought wearily. "I have to go out."

"What? For long?"

He looked at Lord Jim who gazed blankly back.

"I don't know. You'd better not wait. Help yourself to the pizza if you fancy it."

"I brought a pie," she said as if this signified something special, irrevocable, like a marriage vow. In fact, thought Joe, there was something religious in the way she held it out before her.

Lord Jim reached out and broke off a piece which he wordlessly put into his mouth. Alice looked at him in fear and amazement.

"I've got to go," said Joe desperately. "Urgent business."

He moved towards the door, putting on his jacket.

"Will I see you later?" asked Alice.

"I don't know. Perhaps. I'm sorry. Do help yourself to the pizza."

He went through the door ahead of Lord Jim who, surprisingly, paused and looked back.

"Nice pie," he said.

This time the rendezvous was more in keeping

with what Joe had envisaged on Saturday. Lord Jim led him into the back door of an old run-down pub in a section of town scheduled for demolition in the near future. Mine host was a thin, taut-skinned man of about thirty-five with a sickle-shaped scar on his cheek. Beside him Lord Jim looked like the laughing cavalier.

They crossed the bar-room, the kind of drinking quarters to which sawdust would have been a lux-urious addition, and went through another door into what seemed to be a storeroom. Despite the broad daylight outside, it was gloomy in here. The single-paned window high in the wall had had an extractor fan let into it which cut its transluminary powers by half, and the layer of grime and cobwebs over the remaining glass almost completed the job. Barrels and crates were strewn around and the place reeked of stale beer.

A bare bulb dangled from a frayed wire and even as Joe looked at it, it was switched on.

"Hello, Joe, glad you could come."

Cess came into the room and sat down on the one chair.

"Sit down, Joe."

Joe perched himself gingerly on a beer-crate.

"Right," said Cess. He reached up behind him and pulled the cord of the fan. Surprisingly it whirled into action at once.

"Fumes," said Cess. "They gather in a place like this."

"Why do we?" asked Joe.

"What?"

"Gather in a place like this?"

"Funny," said Cess. He didn't sound sincere, thought Joe, watching with fascination as the vor-tex of the fan-blades sucked towards it a couple of thin lines of a cobweb which had been spun across the corner of the window.

"I'm sorry," said Joe, not sure what he was apologizing for.

"Right," said the ginger man. "Just think on. I'm doing you a favour. I'm giving you a chance to collect plenty. With no risk, not to you, any road."

"What do you mean?" asked Joe. Suddenly he saw a gleam of light. "You mean, you wouldn't want me . . ."

"To go on the job with us?" asked Cess in disgust. "I'd rather take Lord Jim's old Betty."

Joe looked with new interest at Lord Jim, in whose craggy features he seemed to detect for the first time something other than blank menace. His wife? Mother? It was unimaginable. It was certainly unaskable.

"What we want from you, Joe, is your expertise. That's it. Your advice. Your considered opinion. Nothing more. That's all we would expect from your sort."

He nodded sagely at his own psychological insight.

My sort! thought Joe indignantly. This low bloody criminal's condescending to me!

"Look, Cess," he said, trying not to sound too ingratiating. "Just exactly what do you want me to do?"

Play for time. There was nothing criminal about talking. Was there? Or could they get you for conspiracy even if no physical attempt at the crime had been made? They'd have to prove it. Tape-recordings of conversations, that sort of thing.

He looked uneasily round the room. Anything could be concealed among these ill-stacked beer crates. But it was hardly likely. His gaze drifted to the fan. The frail strands of cobweb were hanging on against the sucking and tugging of the air-stream. Suddenly Joe felt a great deal of sympathy with the web. Like himself, it was struggling for survival. But play for time. The fan couldn't suck for ever.

Cess lit a cigarette.

"What room's next to the Banqueting Hall?"

Joe did not need to be told where they were.

"To the east the Long Gallery. To the west the Fountain Room."

"How do you get into the Banqueting Hall?"

"Through either of the rooms I've mentioned. Or via the service door which fits flush into the panelling beside the fireplace."

"Where does that lead?"

"Into a long corridor, down a flight of stairs, and eventually to the kitchens."

Cess drew on his cigarette and glanced down. Suddenly Joe realized he was reading the questions from a piece of paper resting on his knee. It was a kind of *viva voce* examination.

"What's on your left as you go into the Music Room?"

"You mean, through the Green Chamber door?"

Cess momentarily looked uneasy.

"Yeah. I suppose so."

Joe was surprised to find he was beginning to enjoy himself.

"On the left?" he said musingly. "Well, now. On the wall is a large and, to my taste, rather ugly painting, artist unknown, early eighteenth-century Dutch school probably. It depicts Orpheus being torn to pieces by the Bacchantes. Evidently, like the good trouper he was, he kept on playing to the bitter end. Below the painting, about five feet from the wall, is a harpsichord, again eighteenth-century, manufactured by Jacob Kirkman in 1777. Moving to the centre of the room, we first encounter, rather discordantly I always feel in a place of melody, a rather tatty Turkish silk carpet, brought back by the sixth lord from his post-Byronic eastern tour in 1832. A couple of Victorian music stands and a chair which claims a pedigree but might well be a forties Woolworth's, are grouped around a beautiful bass viol, made by Barak Norman in 1723. Shall I go further?"

Cess didn't answer but glanced down at his piece of paper once more.

"How many windows has the library?"

"Which library?"

Cess examined him coldly to see if he was trying to be funny. Apparently satisfied, he looked at his paper again.

"You mean there's more than one library?"

"Oh yes. There's the main library, which is what all the visitors troop through. But there's a smaller version in the private apartments. It's called the Book Room, it's a kind of study. Not that any of that lot seem to do any studying," he added gloomily. "But that's where all the best stuff is kept."

"Books, you mean?"

"What else?"

"This is in the private apartments? But you've been in it?"

Too late, Joe began to suspect he had been foolish in appearing so knowledgeable. This had been a heaven-sent chance to appear ignorant, slow, unreliable. Instead of which, seduced by the appeal to his expertise, he had gone even further than the questions required. They had been based simply on a tourist's eye-view of the house. He remembered now the unprecedented diligence with which Mickey Carter had taken notes. But he, Joe

Askern, expert, had stepped off the beaten track purely to show off to Cess Carter, criminal.

"Just once," he said. "I had a peep. Nothing more."

There might still be time to retrieve lost ground. The cobweb strands still held out defiantly against the onslaught of the air.

"You mean you pushed open a door and looked in?"

"That's it. A long time ago."

"How do you know all the best stuff's there, then?"

Not an easy one. As a child, in order to avert the possible bullying attentions of older boys, Joe recalled sometimes letting his jaw sag in an attempt to look a bit simple. It had never worked, but it seemed not a bad idea now.

"I was told."

"Who by? Your mate, the head steward, whatsizname, Laidlaw?"

"It might have been."

Cess looked at him coldly.

"I think it was. I think he probably took you on a private tour of the place sometime when the bloody Trevigores were frigging about on their Mediterranean yacht. He's a good mate, then? That helps a lot."

No, thought Joe. Not Jock. I'm not getting Jock mixed up in this.

"No," he said out loud. "I hardly know him at all."

Cess ignored him and looked down at his piece of paper again. He seemed to have lost the place. Again the thought touched Joe's mind that Carter was not the leading man in this affair. But even if the big brain was not his, he was sharp enough for the business in hand.

"What about alarms?"

"Pardon?"

"Alarms. You know, those things which go ring-ring when you touch what you shouldn't."

"What the hell should I know about alarms?"

Suddenly the black-stone ring was pressed up tight against his nose and Cess's awful Indian-brave face was only six inches away.

"Don't get cocky, Sir. Whatever else you do, never get cocky. Right?"

For once Joe's inner voice was answering in accents even less heroic than the hoarse vibrations from his vocal cords.

"No, no, never, never, no I won't. I promise, please, please, cross my heart and hope to die, Cess, sir, Mr. Carter, touch my forelock, kiss your bum, anything.

"Right," he croaked out loud.

"Good." Carter retreated to his chair. It seemed to Joe that the cobweb was weakening and must be ripped apart any moment now.

"Now, lad, you know your way around the place, you probably know everything in it. We'll come to that in a moment. But you're not going to tell me you haven't noticed other things. Wires, switches, junction boxes, alarm cases. And don't tell me they wouldn't be visible in the big rooms. Not at a glance perhaps, but they'll be there. And in the corridors. And in the steward's quarters where you sit and chat with your mates. You've probably even seen the control board and the master switches. Security's part of Laidlaw's job. Don't say he hasn't talked about it. We all like to talk about our jobs."

There was an ironic accent in his voice. He's right, thought Joe. It was worked out. They knew I'd talk myself into trouble if they set me off.

Worse still, he was right too about Jock Laidlaw and the alarm system. Joe had talked about it, or rather listened to Jock talking. He had seen the whole lay-out. But he had no intention of admitting this.

"No," he said. "Believe me, Cess, I don't know a thing about it. All right, I've probably noticed a few alarms about the place, but that doesn't make me an expert. No, I'm afraid you've backed the wrong horse."

He paused, half-expecting a repeat of Carter's physical threats, but the ginger man seemed to have lost interest. He was studying his paper once more.

"Not to worry, Joe," he said finally. "You'll be able to brush up your memory when you go back to the place."

"No!" said Joe in a sudden panic. "You said you didn't want . . ."

"Shut up! God, you make a bloody noise, don't you!" said Carter in disgust. "I don't mean on the job. I mean, you're going back there on another official visit. Only this time you're going to look at more than the pretty pictures."

"I can't!" said Joe.

"Look, lad. We want to get into the place without making a sound, go straight to the best stuff, pick it up without rousing the neighbourhood and get out likewise. You're a key man at every stage. So don't tell me you can't!"

"I meant, I can't arrange another official visit. Not so soon, I mean. We were only there last week."

"That's all right," said Carter, unconcerned. "No hurry. Not this Saturday. Saturday after will do. You fix it. It might look a bit odd if you turn up just by yourself. But surrounded by kids, everyone making notes, great, eh? We'll let you have a list of what we want. Right?"

He glanced at his watch.

"Have to leave you now, Joe. But don't worry. Everything'll be all right."

He reached forward and patted Joe's knee reassuringly.

"This is a big one, Joe. The biggest. We're not rushing at it. There's a bit more than school clocks in it for us all, eh? By the way, here's a bit of yours in advance. Call it a consultant's fee!"

He produced a wad of notes, counted off ten fivers and tucked them into Joe's breast-pocket.

"Buy that lass of yours some scent. Miss Cohen, isn't it? I once knew a Cohen who ran a chain of betting shops in the Smoke. No relative, I suppose? Anyway I hear she wasn't pleased with you this morning."

Mickey, of course. Little bastard, thought Joe without heat. His main feeling was one of qualified relief. Things were not too bad. Yet. At the worst, his participation (if it came to that) was going to be in the background. And once again he had been given a breathing space. Time for something to come up.

He glanced up. The cobweb strands had survived.

Carter rose.

"Right. Let's be off."

He reached up and pulled the string which stopped the extractor fan.

"Bloody filthy this place," he said fastidiously. And with a swift grab of his left hand pulled the filaments of the web down from the window.

They went through into the bar together. It was now past opening time and a couple of men were sitting at a corner table. Joe thought he recognized them as Carter's companions in the Bell the night of the PTA meeting.

"We'll be in touch," said Carter, and he and Lord Jim moved over to join the others.

Outside Joe was surprised to find it was still broad daylight. Somehow it seemed out of keeping. He breathed in deep. It was good to be out in the open again, even if the open consisted of a dingy back-street. But as he walked away from the pub, his sense of freedom began to seem more and more illusory. And he saw once more with his mind's eye Cess's hand casually clawing at the thin strands of the web.

CHAPTER VIII

Joe felt little incentive to go home. Neither Alice nor a frozen pizza any longer appealed. He would have to do something about Alice. The pizza wouldn't keep for ever either. And the blue Cortina still bothered him. But at the moment all he wanted to do was walk and think, or preferably just walk. He set off towards the town-centre.

He found himself making absurd bargains with fate.

If I reach that blue door in seventy paces, everything will be all right. If the next car I see has two vowels on its number plate ... if I meet a girl wearing yellow stockings ...

He needed a drink. The blue door (which he had reached in ninety-five paces despite lengthening his stride absurdly over the last fifty yards) was the saloon bar entrance of the George and Dragon, a pub he had used regularly till one night with Vernon he had put a drunken dart through the cash register. He went in.

"Small scotch," he said to the barman who looked at him suspiciously. Joe nonchalantly turned his back and leaned against the bar. The room was almost empty—it was still early. An elderly couple sat in silent disunion by the empty fireplace and in the window-seat outlined against the glow of the low-sinking sun was a solitary woman.

She turned her head, saw him, stood up uncertainly.

It was Cynthia.

Joe made for the door.

"Hey!" said the barman, banging the whisky glass on the bar.

"Joe," said Cynthia, coming forward.

"That'll be sixteen pence," said the barman loudly.

Joe turned, sorted out his money, set it on the bar and threw the whisky down his throat.

"Can I talk to you?" asked Cynthia.

Joe replaced the glass on the counter.

"Good evening," he said and made for the door. Cynthia followed him out and struggled to keep up with him as he lengthened his stride down the street.

"I want to explain," she puffed, her block heels cracking loudly against the pavement.

Joe stopped.

"Listen, love," he said. "There's no need to explain. I understand. There's nothing for you to explain. Only get this. It won't work again, not again. I'm sober this time, so take your overblown charms elsewhere."

For a moment he thought she was going to swing her handbag at his head, but finally she relaxed and shrugged.

"I just wanted to say I was sorry," she said.

Immediately he felt guilty. Here I go again, he thought. Cess and Lord Jim may scare the pants off me, but show me a classroom full of kids or a woman by herself and I'll let you see what courage is.

Cynthia had turned away and was about to move off. Suddenly she swung round to him and bent her head forward so that her solidly lacquered blonde hair fell forward like a helmet round her face.

"Give us a light," she said.

"You haven't got a cigarette," said Joe surprised. "What's the matter?"

"Just someone I don't want to meet."

Joe looked round. Walking in their direction on the other side of the street was a familiar figure.

It was Mrs. Carter, Cess's wife.

"Does she know you?" he whispered.

"I know her."

Strangely touched by this display of sensitivity, Joe leaned forward in his turn and put a cigarette into Cynthia's mouth. Mrs. Carter passed them by without a glance.

"Thanks," said Cynthia. She turned to go once more.

"Hang on," said Joe. "Look, what did you want to say to me?"

"I don't know really. Just that, the other night, all that, well I didn't want to do it, that's all."

"Why did you do it then?"

She shrugged.

"I don't know. I had to. I was asked to do an escort job on you. I didn't know how it was going to turn out though. I just had to get you back to your flat drunk. I was a bit drunk myself by then, so it didn't seem too bad an idea to carry on from there like we did."

She looked at him sideways to see his reaction.

"No," he said, smiling reminiscently, "it wasn't too bad at the time."

She smiled widely at him in relief.

"I'm sorry about the photos, understand me. But you're a real one when you get going, aren't you?"

Joe laughed out loud, faintly flattered.

"Am I? You helped a bit, I'd say."

He looked at her seriously for a moment.

"Look, Cyn, you're not here because you've been told, are you? This isn't another set-up?"

He glanced over his shoulder as though expecting to see Chubb lurking close with his camera.

"No!" said Cynthia indignantly. "It's bloody not."

Joe was inclined to believe her. It would have needed more than good organization to be waiting for him in a pub he had had no intention of visiting till a couple of minutes earlier. He made up his mind.

"Right then," he said. "I'll buy you a drink if you're not doing anything."

She looked at him speculatively for a moment.

"Where?" she asked.

"It'll have to be close. I'm on foot."

"That's not a very good idea," she said holding up a set of car-keys. "Be my guest."

"All right. In that case, what about having a bite to eat as well and driving out to the Golden Calf just off the Bakewell Road? Do you know it?"

"I don't think so. Show me."

The reason I am doing this, Joe told himself as he squeezed down beside Cynthia in the tiny Fiat she had led him to, is that this woman might let me have some useful information about Carter and Jim. I've got to clutch at any straw.

But he was very conscious of the pressure of her thigh against his and clutching at straws seemed a most inapposite metaphor.

The Golden Calf was an old country pub which served excellent steaks in the bar. Eventually it would become the victim of its own success and start having pretensions to restaurant status. But the couple of times Joe had been there, the happy balance between local pub-goers and visiting eaters had still been preserved.

With a shock he recalled that it had been Maggie who had first introduced him to the place.

So what? he asked himself. We never really got anywhere. It's hardly desecrating a holy memory or anything like that.

But he still felt a pang compounded of guilt and nostalgia as the Fiat bumped over the uneven surface of the pub car-park.

It had been a silent ride. Memories of their last encounter still hung between them and their conversation had been inconsequential, almost stilted. Joe was beginning to wonder if this had been such a good idea after all as he helped Cynthia out of the car. The physical contact involved reassured him a little, but as they walked over to the pub, the sight of half a dozen sports-cars scattered around the park and sounds of music coming from the building gave him new cause for worry.

His worst fears were realized when they entered the bar. Since his last visit several months earlier the lighting had been diluted by several hundred watts, the tables had sprouted romantic old bottles encrusted with candle-wax, a wall had been knocked down, and in the extra space so gained a shallow platform had risen up which bore a small electric organ and a funny little man who was playing it. In front of the platform on a tiny rectangle of polished floorboards (specially laid over the old stone floor) three or four couples were dancing.

"Have you booked, sir?" asked a rather plain young woman whom he remembered as the landlord's daughter.

"No," he said. "I'm afraid not. I'd be grateful if you could squeeze us in."

His irony was ignored which was a pity. In the past she'd always been good for a laugh.

"This is nice, Joe," said Cynthia when they were seated. She looked around with what seemed to be genuine pleasure and smiled warmly as the plain girl returned with a menu and lit the candle in the bottle.

The music stopped. One of the dancers clapped twice. The little man ignored him.

"I say, you, chappie," called a willowy young man with a gaucho moustache. "Play us . . . *thing* . . . you know."

"What on earth is *thing*, darling?" asked a young girl at the next table, with the kind of upper-class projection which assumes the hearer is two streets away.

"You know. *Thing*. If *you* don't know what *thing* is, my lovely, who on earth does?" replied the gaucho, whose clothes seemed to match his whiskers.

His *bon mot* evoked appreciative laughter from several areas of the room. Most of the clientele, Joe decided, must have arrived together in the awful gaggle of sports-cars he had noticed outside.

"Would you like something to drink, sir?" asked the plain girl.

"What about my whisky, dear?" called the gaucho. "Little bit of service, eh?"

Confused, the plain girl looked round.

"I don't think you ordered anything, Jule," said another rather epicene young man.

"Didn't I? Well, I thought about it hard enough. You there, Semprini, why aren't you playing *thing*?"

"Two scotches. One with water, one with ginger," said Joe.

"You remembered!" said Cynthia satirically.

"It's one of the few things I do remember," said Joe. "What would you like to eat?"

She glanced at the menu and pulled a face.

"Christ, what do they do? Boil everything in virgin's water!"

Joe grinned back at her.

"Things have gone up a bit since last time I was here."

"Not to worry, love," she said. "We'll go dutch."

"That's how we started last time," he said. "No, I asked you here. I'll pay. The plain, unadorned steaks used to be very good. I can't speak for the stuff with fancy names as that's a recent apparition."

"Cess likes a nice bit of steak," she said inconsequentially. The name fell between them like a garter at a church fete. The wad of fivers in Joe's breast-pocket suddenly pressed hard against his heart. They had been much in his mind since leaving Cess and Lord Jim and he had made a firm resolve not to spend. The issue wasn't merely moral, though the thought was very strong in his mind that whatever help he might find himself giving to Carter must never be paid for. In the eyes of the law, a blackmail victim might receive some sympathy; a paid accomplice never. But in addition to this excellent reason for either returning the money or at least preserving it untouched was his suspicion that the notes might be stolen and perhaps traceable. Another link in the chain of criminality by which Cess was hoping to bind him fast. Perhaps they were even forged. Less likely; Cess would hardly want him to run such a large risk of coming to the notice of the police.

"Was the other night Cess's idea?" he asked casually after they had ordered.

"It wasn't mine!" she replied defensively.

"No. Of course not. I didn't mean that. I just wondered if Cess was the sole originator of the plan."

She looked at him suspiciously.

"Why shouldn't he be?"

"No reason. I just thought it a bit odd that he should use you, that's all. He seemed, well, fond of you in his own way."

"Cess doesn't own me!" she snapped.

"The way the other night worked out, it might appear he did," he said quietly.

She put down her knife and fork and for a moment he thought she was going to do something violent like marching out of the restaurant after thrusting a medium rare entrecote up his nose.

Instead she picked up her napkin and covered the lower part of her face, gesturing to the door with her eyes.

"Pig," she said.

"I'm sorry," began Joe.

"Not *you*. Bogey. Cop. Policeman. Just come in."

Joe shrugged, not even bothering to glance round.

"So what? We're entitled to be here."

He felt less casual than he tried to appear and considered heading for the loo and flushing the fivers out of his life for ever.

"Cess might not like us to be seen."

If that was all that was worrying her, he felt relieved.

"He didn't seem to mind the other night."

"No," said Cynthia thoughtfully. "He didn't," and returned to her steak.

Joe glanced round now, expecting to see a village bobby checking that everything was in order. What he saw instead hit him like an expertly delivered combination punch, a right to the heart and a left to the head.

The head blow was the man. It was Sergeant Prince looking incredibly dapper in a light grey suit and pale pink shirt with matching tie. His prematurely white hair gave him an air of considerable distinction. He might have been an old-style Hollywood actor, certain of admiring recognition and instant service.

The heart-blow was the woman he was escorting to their table.

It was Maggie.

Joe kept on staring as she took her seat, her back to him, at the other side of the room. Prince moved round the table and, as he sat down, noticed Joe. He smiled and waved, saying something to Maggie who glanced round briefly, her face expressionless.

Bitch! thought Joe. Coming here of all places. And with him!

Unfair, he added, trying to be reasonable. Sentimental memories didn't stop *me* coming here. And she could hardly know that I'm not exactly *en rapport* with the fuzz at the moment.

But Prince might have a feeling for these things. This thought was worrying. This was the second time. First the golf-club, now this. And Maggie had seen him with Cynthia. That didn't count. Did it? Not unless she mentioned it to Prince. But she wouldn't do that. Why should she? Not when it meant revealing she'd been stood up.

And God knows what the watcher in the blue Cortina had seen.

He glanced round again. Maggie and the sergeant were in close conversation.

"Know them, do you?" asked Cynthia.

"Yes."

"Her as well?"

"Slightly."

Cynthia pushed her plate away from her, unfinished.

"I'd better watch my figure," she said. As though she meant it literally, she unbuttoned the rather loose woollen cardigan she was wearing, took it off and draped it over her chair. Underneath she was wearing a matching jumper, entirely lacking in its fellow's looseness. Her breasts swelled magnificently against the material and the stitching at the apex of the V-neck looked to be in considerable hazard.

Even Maisie Uppadine would be hard pushed to compete with these mature orbs, thought Joe, and the thought brought to mind his poem (*his* now; Mickey Carter's inaugural lines were totally assimilated in the artistic whole, he felt; like Eliot's technique in The Waste Land.)

He found he was staring fixedly at Cynthia's bosom. She didn't seem to mind. But it had attracted other attention as well. The gaucho was leaning over the table, smiling winningly.

"Forgive the intrusion," he said, "but would the lady care to dance?"

The organist had resumed his electronic whining some time earlier.

"I don't think so. Not in between courses," said Joe.

"I asked the lady," said the gaucho, leaning closer to Cynthia.

"Piss off, sonny," said Cynthia without heat.

"Come on, Julian, old son," said the epicene young man who seemed to be wearing a skirt. He pushed the gaucho back towards his own table.

"Sorry, darlings," he said with a flashing smile at Joe. "He's overcompensating for his impotence."

The gaucho turned, not to protest, but explain.

"It's Petula," he said with drunken assurance, nodding at Cynthia. "Used to do things with an Alsatian in that smelly club in Fulham. Don't recognize the face but the bristols are unmistakable."

Joe half-rose.

"Leave it, love," said Cynthia. "I'll have the chocolate pud."

"Nonsense, Jule," said Epicene good-naturedly. "Probably a colonial bishop's daughter here for the hols. Don't spoil things, there's a nice old eunuch."

Joe concentrated his attention on unravelling the small, tight ball of anger and resentment which was being wound up in his belly. He might have succeeded if the gaucho had not shaken off his friend and returned.

"Bishop's daughter," he said solemnly. "Bless you."

He picked up Joe's drink, dipped his fingers in it and began flicking droplets of scotch down Cynthia's cleavage, intoning, "In nomine Patrii, Filii et . . ."

He got no further. Joe caught him in the stomach with a round-arm left and gasped in agony as his hand almost broke off at the wrist. The gaucho doubled up most satisfactorily and was violently sick over the table, causing Cynthia to leap back out of the line of fire.

Joe was surprised to see she did not look in the least grateful for his intervention.

"Christ Almighty," she said, gathering together her things. "Let's go."

She attempted to push Joe towards the door but their way was blocked by a white-haired figure, no longer looking merely distinguished, but now very professional and businesslike.

"Hold it, Mr. Askern," he said. "What's the trouble?"

"No trouble, Sergeant, we're just going," said Cynthia.

"Are you all right, Jule?" cried a large square

girl, one of the group of people who had gathered round.

"Oh, oh, oh," groaned the gaucho.

"Sergeant? Are you a policeman? How ducky," said Epicene. "This nasty follow has done poor Jule an injury."

"What happened?" asked Prince.

"Jule was having a bit of fun. No, no, no," said Epicene brushing aside Joe's attempted protest, "just fun. Rather objectionable perhaps, but fun nonetheless, and certainly no cause for this kind of brutality."

His voice became quite shrill as he finished. Joe rubbed his wrist and looked at him longingly.

"You hit him, Mr. Askern?" said Prince.

"Yes," said Joe. "But . . ."

"But me no buts," said Epicene. "Aren't you going to arrest him?"

"Will your friend wish to bring charges, do you think?" asked Prince in an official voice.

Epicene looked questioningly at the square girl. She shook her head.

"Daddy wouldn't like it. Just tell this yobbo to bugger off with his tart before Jule returns to us."

The gaucho fixed Joe with a gaze of pure hatred. "Oh, oh, oh," he said, still holding his stomach.

"You are—?" said Prince to the square girl.

"I'm his sister, God help me."

"Name, please," said the sergeant patiently.

"Trevigore. Helen Trevigore and this is my brother Julian."

"Trevigore?" said Prince. "Any relation to Lord Trevigore?"

"Our father; which art in bed and will remain there undisturbed, I hope."

There was a round of high-bred laughter. Prince

turned to Joe and took him a couple of paces aside.

"I think it'll all smooth itself over if you push off now, Mr. Askern. Word of advice, don't be so keen to swing your fists next time, eh?"

"You haven't asked for my version, Sergeant," said Joe, keeping his voice low with difficulty.

"You did hit him? Yes. I saw it. Look it's not worth it, sir. Just push off, eh?"

"Because his name's bloody Trevigore, is that it?" snarled Joe.

"No," said Prince patiently.

"Balls," said Joe. "Dirty great . . ."

"Come on, Joe," said Cynthia, taking his arm. He glanced across at Maggie who lifted her chin fractionally, returned his gaze for a second, and looked away. The organist, who had stopped playing for a couple of minutes, started again. Joe looked round the semi-circle of unfriendly faces. Some of them weren't even unfriendly, just impersonally curious, as though he were in a glass cage.

He bent over the gaucho who was still in some discomfort.

"Fancy a dance, Jule, old son?" he said. "They're playing *thing*."

At the door he met the plain girl. He peeled a fiver off the wad given to him by Cess and put it into her hand.

"Harpics all round," he said.

It wasn't a very good exit line and he sat in silence in the car on the return journey, composing better ones. He didn't feel like talking and Cynthia accepted his mood. Her only comment on the incident was when she said musingly with no trace of accusation in her voice, "Nights out with Cess often end in a punch-up, but I'd have bet against it tonight."

She dropped him in the town-centre, neither offering nor receiving an invitation for the evening to be continued elsewhere.

"Thanks," she said, again without irony.

"Thank you for the ride," said Joe. "You'll be seeing Cess? Give him a message. Tell him it'll be a real pleasure to help. A real pleasure."

As he strode away down the darkling streets to home, he really believed it.

CHAPTER IX

On the next trip to Averingerett it poured down. They went in a twelve-seater minibus belonging to the LEA and even then only seven children turned up. Mickey Carter sat next to Maisie and kept her giggling most of the way with a series of suggestive line drawings on the steamed-up windowpanes.

He had a talent for it, Joe observed gloomily through the driving-mirror. Perhaps sufficient to lure him away from the erratic trail of his father's footsteps. He'd talk to Godspur, the art man. And Mrs. Carter.

The trip had not proved too difficult to organize. Cess had been adamant that he must use a school visit as his cover and the story he had settled on was that a small group of children had not had time fully to pursue their chosen lines of research on the previous visit and were now pressing him to take them again.

Solly had been doubtful at first. It was one of his proud boasts that his school always had more of its various allowances left over at the end of the financial year than any other school in the district. What won him over was the realization that a small group ("a dozen at most," Joe had invented hurriedly) could be conveyed in the LEA minibus with Joe driving, thus keeping down expense. But, more importantly, use of the minibus opened up whole networks of unclassified roads which a large coach could not negotiate.

In Joe's pocket rested a route-map which would

have done credit to any army of invasion. Many alternatives were shown, but the recommended route, involving only one ford and a Forestry Commission track, was guaranteed to be the shortest by just under a furlong. Cyril had actually appeared to make a note of the mileage before they set off.

He was going to be disappointed, thought Joe grimly as he headed the minibus along the main road through the torrential rain.

Much of his sense of committal after his encounter with the young Trevigore set had quickly worn off. But a small core of anger still remained which he hoped might see him through. He nursed it carefully. It was all he had.

What I need's a good old Robin Hood syndrome, he thought. Rob the rich to feed the poor. For *poor* read Cess and Lord Jim. And me. Oh yes. And me.

After his initial gesture with the first of Carter's five-pound notes, it had been fairly easy to spend the rest. Joe was not at all certain where it had gone. The only tangible gain he had from the money was a new 4-wood which dispatched balls to impenetrable areas of the course whenever he used it. Every lost ball seemed like the judgment of God.

His relationship with Maggie had returned to a superficial normality. They were coldly polite to each other in public, but she resisted any attempt at a rapprochement. Staff-room gossip had seized eagerly on her friendship with Sergeant Prince and if the experts were to be believed she was seeing a lot of him. Joe's only reference to him brought an immediate scornful reply about pub-brawlers, and the matter was allowed to lie, not dead but uneasily dormant.

Now even the great western façade of Averingerett

failed to work its customary magic. The driving rain didn't help matters, obscuring the clean lines of the building and even absorbing into its own being the majestic jets of the great fountain. But it was more than just a personal reaction to the weather. Rather it was the other way round, Joe felt. The pathetic fallacy in action.

He put it to himself quite bluntly.

I am here to case the joint.

Cess's instructions had been impressive in their own way. Joe was no expert in the techniques of joint-casing, but it seemed to him that this particular scheme of work had been well thought-out and prepared. By Cess? he wondered. He'd have placed Cess as a man of action, working intuitively rather than by thoughtful planning. Yet someone had planned thoughtfully, or he would not be here now, running through the rain for the shelter of the stables arch.

"Hello there, Mr. Askern," said the man collecting the admission money. "Back again?"

"That's right. Just eight of us this time, seven children and me. Is Jock around?"

"I expect he's in his office. Shall I buzz him for you?"

"No, no," said Joe. "I'll drop in later. Come on, kids."

He paused at the edge of the stables arch and peered across the courtyard through the rain. The stable-block through the great archway which now acted as the visitors' entrance, had been converted into the business centre of the house. The estate manager's offices as well as the head steward's room were contained here.

There was no internal connection between the block and the main house, and the route for visitors lay across the courtyard into what had once been the kitchen quarters but was now dignified with the title of entrance hall.

It was into the stable-block that Cess and Lord Jim had tried to force entry on their abortive mission a few weeks earlier, Joe recalled. That sounded a hare-brained scheme, Carter working intuitively rather than from a plan.

Dimly Joe recollected mocking Cess and Lord Jim for their failure. Now he wished heartily they had met with every success that night. Or failed so miserably they had been caught.

Either way, he would never have become involved.

"Aren't we going in?" asked Maisie plaintively. She was wearing a tightly-belted fluorescent purple pvc raincoat along the sweeping curves of which raindrops were doing a wall-of-death act. Joe didn't blame them for clinging.

"Right, across we go. Make a run for it!"

Heads down, they sprinted through the downpour into the shelter of the entrance hall. Here Joe paused and considered his brood. A predictable lot, he thought. Fat Alf Certes and a trio of other misfits who had nothing better to do on a Saturday afternoon. Little Molly Jarvis, who loved him. Mickey Carter, who certainly didn't love him. And Maisie Uppadine, whose motives were much more cloudy. She was certainly not a misfit and could have no difficulty in finding things to do on Saturday or any other day.

The stone floor of the entrance hall echoed hollowly under their feet. He had rarely seen the place so deserted. The rain must have discouraged many visitors and he had noticed the car-park held only a fraction of its normal Saturday quota of cars. The children grouped themselves around him expectantly.

"Now, you all know what you have to do. I shall be making my own way round in about ten minutes so you'll be able to ask me if you want any help about your work. All right? Then off you go. And remember. *Don't touch anything!*"

Ironic, he thought as he watched them troop obediently along the prescribed route up the stairs out of the hall. Here am I, an accessory before the fact of housebreaking, instructing my flock to touch nothing.

But only before the fact, he comforted himself slightly. Once they've had the benefit of my researches, they're on their own.

He recalled with pleasure the horror on Cess's face at the thought of actually taking him on the job, and resolved to fall over a couple of chairs next time they met just to reinforce the impression of general incompetency.

But he had better be competent now. While he hoped with all his heart that Cess and Lord Jim would get their come-uppance, he had no illusions that they would be generous, understanding losers if they suspected he was in any way to blame. He set about his allotted tasks with care.

A good deal of what he had been told to find out, he could have told them without having to revisit the house. Contents of rooms, distances, dimensions, numbers and positions of windows and doors, for instance, and much else. But it was all worth re-checking. And there was much else to do. Types of locks on internal doors and display cabinets, window-fastenings, and above all, Carter wanted every minute piece of information he could glean on the alarm-system.

"A wire, a switch, anything at all, you note it, Joe. It doesn't matter if you don't understand it as long as you let us know."

"But you could do all this yourself," he had protested.

"Oh no. Lord Jim or me poking about would be asking for trouble. You've got a head start, Joe boy. And, most important of all, you can get the inside stuff. Pump your mate Laidlaw for all he's worth. About the alarms, about what happens at night, who's about the place, how many servants live in, when is his bloody lordship in residence. That's another thing you'll see on our list. Get yourself back into the private bit of the house and do your stuff there as well."

"But . . ." Joe had started to protest.

"Do it, Joe," Cess had said softly.

Joe stopped protesting.

The public rooms were easy. Joe made his way round swiftly, exchanging a word or two with stewards he knew, but wasting no time. It was better this way. Once when he paused in the Tapestry Room and thought of Lord Jim bundling together pieces of the exquisite French silk-work like so many nylon stockings he asked himself in horror, *What am I doing?*

Surviving, was the grim answer.

On his way round he over took all the children. Maisie and Mickey stood close together, heads thrown back, silently contemplating an eager Venus chasing a reluctant Adonis across the ceiling of the State Bedroom. Joe went by them without attracting their attention. He had no need to dwell there, he felt. Even Cess could hardly be contemplating stealing a four-poster bed. Only Molly Jarvis held him up with questions about the duties of a lady's maid. She came from a good working-class Tory background and obviously fancied herself all neat and tidy in a nice black and white outfit. Joe was reluctant to leave her with all her illusions, but had to press on, promising to return later.

The reason for his haste was simple, almost noble. He felt a growing reluctance to involve his friend Jock Laidlaw in any aspect of the business. (Business! Crime, he told himself. I must stop talking to myself in euphemisms!) Pumping him for information would be bad enough, but he felt a special reluctance about asking Jock to take him into the private apartments today. In any case, he would probably refuse as the Trevigores were officially in residence, even though Joe had ascertained that most of the party had departed for the day to the North Midlands Horse Trials near Nottingham.

I hope dear Jule gets kicked in the crutch, thought Joe viciously, and Lady Helen wins a prize for the biggest crupper. Whatever that is.

He had a fair recollection of the route by which Jock usually led him to the Book Room. He had no intention of breaking new ground, but wished merely to confirm his recollections. Cess would have to accept that there were limits to his knowledge. As long as he was accurate within those limits, no one could complain.

After a swift glance over his shoulder to make sure he was alone, he stepped over the single-strand barrier at the end of the L-shaped Painted Gallery. The foot of the "L" was thus amputated. Visitors might officially crane their heads round the corner to gawk at two undistinguished chairs and a cracked Grecian urn, but they were allowed no nearer the three doors which opened off this part of the gallery into the private rooms.

It was through the nearest of these that Joe had gone under Laidlaw's supervision and he now gently turned the handle, eager to be through, but careful of what might lie on the other side.

It seemed to be locked.

Behind him he heard a sudden chatter of voices. A gang of sightseers must be approaching the gallery. Forswearing gentleness, he pushed with all his weight against the door.

It was definitely locked.

The voices were very near now. There was hardly time to retreat. In any case if he did, he knew he would not have the nerve to try again elsewhere. Quickly he moved down the foot of the "L" out of the view of anyone coming down the gallery, and approached the next door.

His hand was almost on the handle when it turned itself, as though magically operated. Someone was coming through from the other side.

Three strides took him to the third and final door. He pushed it open as a figure emerged from the door he had just abandoned, stepped through, and only by a great effort of will prevented himself from slamming it shut behind him.

Only when he had finally by infinitesimal degrees let the handle return to its original position did he realize he was trembling from head to foot.

He rested his forehead against the cool woodwork and took three deep breaths. Jesus! Cess was right. He wasn't cut out for this kind of thing.

One last deep breath and he turned. Stretching out before him was a long unadorned corridor, its bareness contrasting strongly with the luxury of the apartments he had just passed through. The room he had intended entering must lie to his right. Once in there on relatively familiar ground, he could make a swift reconnaissance of the four or five rooms Jock had shown him over, then reappear in permitted territory through a small well-shaded door beneath the entrance hall stairs, a door which was only openable from the inside.

All he had to do now was to take the first door to the right.

He set off down the corridor.

The only trouble was that there didn't seem to be a door to the right. In fact the only exits from the corridor were through the door behind him into the Painted Gallery or through the one which lay dead ahead, leading God knows where.

Carefully he pressed his ear to it and listened. Nothing. But nothing meant nothing when you built doors as thick as those at Averingerett. Nor was there a key-hole to peer through to check what lay beyond. It was dangerous. For all he knew, the entire Trevigore family could be sitting at lunch on the other side. Unlikely as they had gone to Nottingham. But it was risky for all that. The wise thing would be to retreat.

Behind him he heard the gallery door slowly open. Whoever had disturbed him before was now re-entering the private sector by this route.

It's like a bloody French farce, he thought humourlessly, all the exits and entrances in full swing, disaster just a hinge away.

Even as he thought, he had acted. Perhaps, he told himself with surprise, I *am* like Cess, intuitive rather than calculating.

He was in a long room, broad enough to be called a gallery rather than a corridor, but a long way from the dignified proportions of the Painted or the Sèvres Galleries. There were three windows in shallow bays looking out over the formal gardens lying to the rear of the house. It was still raining hard, he had time to notice, before turning his mind to the task of choosing which of the three doors opening off the gallery he should go through. He stood, uncertain, unwilling to commit himself. Nothing helped him. Not a sound was to be heard.

I'm at it again. Calculating, he told himself. Let your instincts work.

His unconscious pursuer must be close. All right, instincts, work! But quickly!

Be bloody terrified! Get out of sight! answered his instincts brutally.

He pushed open the nearest door and stepped into a bedroom. Not one of your richly-ornamented-and-four-postered Queen-Anne-slept-here bedrooms but a lived-in or slept-in room, comfortably furnished in a pre-war style which came near to rampant *avant-gardism* in a place like Averingerett. Perhaps even the doors had been brought up to date, for through the one which stood directly opposite that which he had just closed (a draughty arrangement, surely) he distinctly heard voices. Someone was approaching.

Retreat was impossible. Whoever was behind him had probably just entered the gallery and would be very surprised to see him backing out of the bedroom. It was better to take his chances where he stood. No one could be going to spend much time in a bedroom early on a Saturday afternoon. The doors of a large wall-cupboard stood invitingly ajar to the left of the door opposite; it was with a rather comforting back-to-the-womb sense of security that he settled back among the hanging clothes (all male) and saw the outside world reduced to the merest edge of light where the doors met.

I like it in here, he thought. A man could settle down here. A life of meditation, untroubled by income-tax and Onions and lust and Lord Jim. Completely safe.

Unless whoever had just come into the room wanted a change of clothing.

His mind threw-up vivid pictures of the family and their guests, soaken at the horse-trials, returning early eager to get out of their wet togs.

Mulled wine in the mulled-winery in minutes five, Toby, old son!

Right-ho, dear boy. I'll just pop up the Harry stairers to rid me of these damp rags.

Exit, humming Eton Boating Song.

Opens wardrobe door.

Who the hell are you?

I've come to read the meter.

No, that wouldn't do.

Laundry, sir. Just checking your dry-cleaning needs.

Hardly.

You rang, sir?

Better. But why the hell was he being so subservient? If he was going to try a lie, why not lie on the basis of equality?

Toby, my love! Surprise, surprise! Give us a kiss, one for me and one for m'tutor!

Then kick him in the balls and run?

Not the best of recommendations, this, to Cess and his gang. But who the hell wanted to be recommended to that lot anyway? On the contrary, discovery now might have advantages.

Not that it seemed likely to take place. Everything had gone very quiet. Joe sat in the dark, straining his ears. Not a thing. Perhaps it had been a flying visit, perhaps just a chambermaid turning down a silk coverlet or replenishing the warming-pan.

He counted up to two hundred, then slowly pushed the doors open.

And was immediately aware that his previous assessments of the situation had fallen short in two particulars.

Firstly, he had quite ignored the one activity which might well occupy two people in a bedroom for a long period on a wet Saturday afternoon.

Secondly, when sifting through his selection of

excuses for his presence in the room, he had not considered the possibility that he might be known to the discoverer.

In short, the Honourable Julian Trevigore was preparing to have it away on the bed.

The girl involved looked familiar and for one awful moment Joe thought he had strayed into Iris Murdoch country and she was none other than the Hon. Helen Trevigore. But a second look convinced him the resemblance was generic rather than familiar.

Once more Joe found himself faced with a choice. Wait, with the risk of being discovered if Julian felt like a change of gear at the finish of his labours.

Or try to make off under cover of the heavy breathing.

For a moment his desire for escape warred desperately with his hatred of action. He glanced through the crack in the door again. The Hon. Julian, he assessed, wasn't here for a quick plunge but intended to take a long, leisurely dip. Which meant good cover for an escape and a long wait if he held his ground.

That settled it. Choosing his moment carefully, he pushed the doors gently open and began to crawl across the room pausing only when he was in the lee of the bed and attending carefully to the activities above. Getting through the door was the most perilous task; he wanted a moment of maximum inattention.

It seemed to be approaching. The bed creaked in genteel protest, providing an antiphony to the gasps and groans of the hard-struggling pair.

Now! thought Joe. This is the moment.

It might well have been.

Only his progress was impeded by the sudden descent of two closely intertwined naked bodies over the edge of the bed.

"Jesus!" gasped Joe, his breath knocked out of him.

"Ouch!" exclaimed Julian, who seemed to have sustained an injury in the fall.

"Aaahhh!" shrieked the girl whose passion-flushed face had come to rest about three inches from Joe's.

Despite his inferior position, Joe was first up with Julian close behind.

"Who the hell are you?" demanded Julian, as yet sounding more incredulous than angry.

Despite himself, Joe found he was going into his loyal serf routine.

"Just checking, sir," he said, grinning vacantly. "Won't keep you no longer. Just checking on the worm."

He rapped the bedside-table unconvincingly, thought *stuff it!* touched his forelock, and made for the door.

"I know you!" said Julian. "It's you! Isn't it?"

"Good show, old thing!" laughed Joe. "Might have known you'd see through me. Well, mustn't keep you from your fun. 'Bye!"

He turned to the door and was surprised to find his face pushed hard against it and his left arm forced painfully up his back. The Hon. Julian was not as weedy as he looked. In fact, thought Joe, to be quite fair, unclothed he was quite a well set-up young man.

"Shall I ring the police, Jule?" asked the girl, affecting total boredom after her initial fright.

"No!" spluttered Joe into the panelling.

"You're that prick in the pub, aren't you? The one with the tart. What the hell are you up to here?" demanded Jule.

"Isn't he just a burglar, dear?" asked the muscular girl, who had lit a cigarette and spread herself across the bed once more.

"I don't know? Are you, rat-face?"

The pain in his arm increased as Julian pressed harder.

Oh dear, thought Joe. He didn't want to get into a fight. On the other hand there were limits. Julian must be made to realize that a naked man is peculiarly susceptible.

He stepped back gently on to his toes. At least, gentleness was his intention. The result was spectacular.

"Aaahh!" shrieked Julian in agony, hopping backwards till he lost his balance and crashed to the floor.

The girl on the bed was obviously convinced this was the prelude to a murderous attack. Her aplomb fled, and her naked pose was shattered. One arm crossed her breasts, her other hand pressed hard down on her pubes and she threw back her head to produce a noise like a Cumberland hound-trailer calling his dog home.

Joe turned to go. Flight was foolish. He had seven children and a minibus to collect before he could go anywhere. But his ears couldn't take much more of this noise.

He was prevented by the door being flung open in his face.

A stocky, grey-haired man with a determined block of a jaw barred his way.

"Hello, Jock," said Joe.

"Hello, Joe. What the hell's going on?"

For answer Joe stood back to reveal the scene behind him. Jock would vouch for him, he thought moodily, but the Hon. Julian would hardly let the matter rest there. Jock looked in silence at the two naked figures before him. Slowly the noise died down.

"Laidlaw," began Julian waving a threatening fist at Joe. "Laidlaw, grab this bastard and call the police. No, I'll call the police. You just grab him. He attacked me."

Jock did not move but looked with distaste at the naked pair. There was a strong Puritanical streak in his make-up and his loyalties were to the house, not the family.

"Good day, Mr. Julian," he said finally. "And good day to you too, Mrs. Throgmorton."

There was the gentlest of stresses on the last two words.

And Joe knew he was saved.

Ten minutes later, his explanation and apology having been, on the surface at least, accepted, he was in the head steward's room, drinking scotch with a Guinness chaser.

Jock too seemed to accept the slightly different version of the story Joe offered to him.

"I just wanted to do some work in the Book Room. I knew the family were out, you weren't around, so I set off myself and got lost. Sorry."

Jock studied him carefully for a long moment.

Finally, "Aye," he said thoughtfully. "Another wee drop?"

Joe felt in no mood to carry on with his under-cover researches, but ironically, without being in the least pressed, Jock seemed bent on offering him just the kind of information Cess had told him to get. Information about the return from exhi-bition-loan of certain treasures, about the modifi-cation of certain security procedures, and above all about the alarm-system.

"This is the nerve centre of the operation," said Jock proudly, leading Joe into a small, windowless room where a junior steward sat reading a maga-zine before a large panel of switches and lights.

"Christ!" said Joe, looking around in surprise. "This is far more complicated than it used to be."

"Aye, well. It needs to be, of course. We thought we might as well make a job of it," said Jock smugly.

"Needs to be? But why now, specially?" asked Joe.

Jock looked at him in surprise.

"You mean you don't know? Man, I thought you'd surely know! Have you not seen the work that's been going on up the Great Park?"

"Well, I noticed something being done up by the Blue Grotto last time. But I haven't been into the park today. Why?"

He began to laugh as Jock told him. He laughed all the way home. Twice he nearly steered the minibus off the road as his shoulders rocked with internal amusement. He laughed when Cyril met him at the school to check his mileage which to his chagrin was five miles more than it needed to be.

And when he switched off the light that night and lay down in his bed, lowering his defences against all the mole-like thoughts which during past weeks had come burrowing busily through the dark, for the first time he greeted them without worry and fell asleep with a smile on his lips.

CHAPTER X

"Not Lines. LI-ONS," said Joe carefully.

He had chosen his moment. He wished to savour it to the full, a savour none the worse for being spiced with a dash of fear at the possible violence of Carter's reaction.

It was three days since the last trip to Averingerett. He had expected to be summoned earlier and had been disappointed when Sunday and Monday had passed with no word. But he had come home about eight o'clock on Tuesday evening to find Lord Jim in the hallway discussing his whereabouts with a rather fearful Alice.

Now they were back in the pub store-room where the last meeting took place, only this time there were three others present. Two of them were the men Cess had joined in the bar on the previous occasion, the third he had never seen before. He assumed these constituted the complete Averingerett break-in team.

Soon to be dismantled, he told himself with relief.

They had listened in silence as he gave an outline account of his investigations, going out of his way to hint at real detail of information to come, which indeed he had. He wanted them hooked before he came to the high point.

But as he described the new developments in the control-room, he saw that this in itself was spreading a great deal of despondency amongst those present. They took their cue from Lord Jim, who questioned him in detail about the system, making him repeat several pieces of information.

Seeing the effect he was having on his listeners, Joe racked his memory for details and dredged up a much fuller picture than he thought possible, certainly much fuller than he had intended giving to them.

"You sure?" asked Lord Jim for the fifth or sixth time. "Must have cost 'em a fortune. I don't understand it."

"What's the matter, Jim? Can't we get in?" asked Cess looking worried.

"It'll be a lot harder," grunted Jim. "And take a lot longer."

Cess shot an anxious glance at the newcomer to the group, a little dark-skinned man.

"We'll have all the time in the world," he urged. "The place'll be almost deserted. There's next to no chance of anyone spotting the van parked in those grounds. You take all the time you like, Jim. We'll stroll around and enjoy the view."

He looked around with an unbecoming jocularity to which everyone except the little dark man responded. Even he relaxed a little, however, and Joe decided it was time to speak.

"Yes," he said with a smile. "It'll be nice wandering around the grounds at night. Except if you're worried about lions."

No one spoke for a moment.

"Lines?" said Cess. "What kind of lines?"

"Not lines. LI-ONS," Joe articulated with great clarity. "Lord Trevigore's lions. Now, what do you want to do next? Look at the ground-floor lay-out?"

He knew it was a mistake as soon as he spoke. Cess was across the room, holding him lightly by the lapel, in a split second.

He spoke softly.

"I warned you before about playing clever buggers with me, *Sir*. Now just you tell us, slow and easy, what you're talking about. Else I might break your bloody neck."

"Lions!" Joe heard himself gabbling. "Lions at Averingerett. Like Longleat. He's turning the grounds into a wild-life park and bringing in some lions."

The effect on his hearers was as powerful as he had hoped. Even Cess relaxed his grip and stood back.

"Lots of lions," Joe added with vicious emphasis. "The savagest there are."

"Are you sure?" asked Cess.

"Certain."

The little dark-skinned man stood up.

"That's it," he said with a strong East London accent.

"Sit down, Bertie."

"I don't fancy no lions, Cess," said Bertie.

"Give it a minute, lad," said Cess. Bertie shrugged and sat down.

Cess returned his attention to Joe.

"Details," he said. "When?"

"End of June," said Joe. "They weren't due till later, but they became available. So they're speeding things up."

"I don't fancy them beasts," said Bertie again. "What about you, Killer?"

The man called Killer shook his head.

"Know nowt about 'em. But I reckon them'll need watching."

"They half-killed a man at the other place," said the third man, who didn't seem to have a name. "And he was in a car. Took his arm off."

"He should have kept his window shut," snapped Cess. "But you're all jumping the gun. We know nothing yet. They're not going to have bloody lions roaming about under their windows, are they? Let's make some sense. So give, Joe. Where will they be?"

Joe was ready for this. He fiddled around in his pocket till he found a piece of chalk.

"No," he said. "They won't be directly outside the house, of course. Look. Here's the position."

He stood up, turned a large packing-case on its side and drew a large circle.

"That's the Trevigore grounds," he said. "This bottom quarter-segment is the river."

In the circle near the bottom he drew another circle and inside this an oblong.

"That's the house," he said. "The small circle contains the formal gardens. The rest is the Great Park. Now a barrier is going up right round the Great Park, that is the large circle. That is to keep the animals in. And a similar barrier round the formal gardens. To keep the things out. But between those two barriers, the lions will have complete freedom of movement. Complete freedom."

He spoke with emphasis.

"How the hell does anyone get into the house?" asked the third man suddenly.

"Simple," said Joe enjoying himself. "The road comes down across the river here."

He drew a dotted line.

"The barrier runs about fifty yards the other side of the river. There is a double gate, one on the bridge and one in the barrier. One of these will always be shut. Once you're in you just keep your windows closed and drive straight along to the house, passing through another gate here."

He continued the dotted line straight to the rectangle which indicated the house, then drew another circle, also in dots, between the two unbroken circles.

"That indicates the inner track along which those who wish to see the animals will drive. This will bring them full circle back to the main driveway, where they will either turn left for the exit or right if they also wish to visit the house. That'll cost more, of course."

"Bugger the cost. We weren't going to pay," said Cess irritably.

"This barrier," said Lord Jim, speaking for the first time. "Just what is it?"

Joe sat down again. After his initial scare, he was enjoying himself, but he took care not to let it show.

"Basically a thorn hedge. Some was already in place. A good deal has been transplanted from elsewhere in the park. And some has been newly planted. Eventually the aim is an impenetrable hedge, at least ten feet high and six feet wide."

"Eventually," said Lord Jim. "What about now?"

"Now it's being re-inforced with wire, mesh and barbed,' said Joe. "Round the inside of the hedge run a couple of lightly electrified wires, just to warn the animals off. And a third wire runs through the hedge itself and this responds to any fairly violent touch, such as something trying to force its way through, by setting off an alarm in the stables control-house. A steward is on alarm duty twenty-four hours a day and an armed Land-Rover patrol is on constant standby. So any sign that anything's trying to get out—or *in*—and they're right on the spot."

"That just about wraps it up, my loves," said Bertie, making for the door. "Who's for a wet before I leave?"

"Hang on," said Cess.

"What for? Little Lord Fauntleroy here's asking questions about getting into the park, isn't he?

Forget it, Cess. Even if you could get through that hedge with all the gear and without being shot, who in hell's going to walk a couple of miles with a lot of oversize cats suffering from night starvation? I'm off."

The other two, Killer and the Third Man, both made agreeing movements. Only Cess and Lord Jim remained still.

It's breaking up! thought Joe gleefully. They'll have to abandon the whole bloody thing.

"We could bring it forward," said Cess without conviction.

"Don't be daft! I've got my outlet timed for July five. It's a very delicate arrangement. They don't want the stuff before then—you know that. This kind of gear's got to move like a peppererd ferret till it's out of harm's way, hasn't it? You know that. Do *you* want to sit on it for a month? Bloody right you don't. No more do I want to be carting it around with me. In any case, a lot of the stuff we want don't come back from this pissing exhibition till the end of June. You said that, son?"

He looked at Joe who nodded affirmation.

"And the family will be in residence till then anyway," Joe added.

"There you are. Another risk. No, it stinks to me. Pity. It hasn't been cheap, not even this far."

"Hang on," said Cess again. "Two minutes? Right?"

Bertie shrugged and sat down.

"All right."

Cess left the room. To do what? wondered Joe. Check on his information? Report back? Perhaps he didn't have the authority to cancel without consultation. Then who did?

"Here, tell us again about that pair falling out of bed!' said Bertie who had been inordinately amused at Joe's account of his misadventure. Feeling light of heart, Joe re-told the tale, with greater relish and additional embellishment this time.

Bertie rolled around with laughter, Killer and Third Man smiled widely. Only Lord Jim was unamused. Bertie nudged him.

"What's the matter, mate? Haven't you been given permission to laugh, then?"

Joe shuddered at the thought of taking such liberties with Lord Jim and waited for an explosion, but before anything could happen Cess returned. He still looked worried, Joe was glad to see.

"Bertie, we'll need a couple of days to work on this," he said.

Bertie looked disbelieving.

"A couple of days?"

"That's right. You can manage that."

"Oh, I can manage it all right. But I don't know if I want to! Look, Cess, I got a reputation. I don't want no cock-up. Now it sounded like you had a nice little thing going here. Someone on the inside almost, like Joe, that helps. And if Jim says he can get into a place, I accept that. But now he's doubtful, isn't he, and that was before he knew about the bleeding lions and the big white hunters pissing about all over the place! It's sounding more like a non-starter every minute. Some of the big boys might manage something, but a small set-up like yours is getting out of its depth."

Joe had to stop himself applauding. It was a beautiful speech, beating anything in Shakespeare. Cess looked annoyed and offended, but was clearly making an effort to keep himself in check.

"Till the end of the week," he urged. "You can spare that, Bertie."

Bertie shrugged.

"Why not?" he said to Joe's disappointment.

"But I won't accept no botched-up job, Cess. It'll have to be watertight before the weekend. Then I'll have to cancel my market."

The meeting broke up and Joe whistled merrily in the car as he drove home. With a bit of luck, his troubles would be over within a very few days. Even the sight of the blue Cortina parked discreetly at the bottom of the street could not take the fine edge off his happiness.

CHAPTER XI

The next day at school Joe felt less optimistic and found himself plunged deep into a melancholy which even a new experimental reversal of the school blouse by Maisie Uppadine could not alleviate. In a fit of abstraction he even told little Molly Jarvis, who loved him, to belt up, and had to spend half an hour piecing together the wreckage. Worse, he suspected Molly went and poured her heart out to Maggie Cohen and his fears seemed to be confirmed when Maggie followed him into the English store-room after lunch.

At least she looked faintly anxious, he thought. Which was a change from the air of cold indifference she had assumed towards him in the past week.

Better still (or so it seemed at first) her anxiety wasn't directed at Molly but himself.

She came straight to the point, not even starting with *it's none of my business but . . .*

"Are you in some sort of trouble, Joe?"

"What had you in mind, Maggie?" he leered, startled.

"Can we forget the clever cracks, Joe? I asked you a question."

Drop in temperature. Watch it, Askern. Why does everyone object so violently to "cleverness"?

"I'm sorry. Seriously, what makes you ask, Maggie? I mean, there's all kinds of trouble. Financial, professional. Emotional."

Slight stress on that word. She doesn't react. Forget it.

Maggie hesitated, but only a second.

"I'm not sure. Police trouble? I was out last night with Maurice . . ."

"Maurice?"

"Sergeant Prince."

"Oh, *that* Maurice."

That was silly. Being clever again. You want to hear this, Askern. This could be bad.

"He mentioned you in passing. Not in confidence, I don't think. I feel he might even have wanted me to drop a hint to you."

Big of him!

There. You kept it in that time.

"About what, for God's sake?"

"Well, something to do with what happened at the Golden Calf the other night, I think. You were mentioned in passing, by Maurice not me, I assure you. And he added something about the people you go around with. It was more the *way* he said it."

Joe's nerves were wearing thin.

"What did he *say*, Maggie? Just tell me that. Not what you think he meant, not what he indicated by winks, nods and masonic signs. Just what he *said*!"

Temperature down to zero now. What the hell!

"He asked if you knew Averingerett well. After I answered, he said, 'Not a place he'd get lost in, then?' Naturally I wasn't greatly interested in talking about *you* on a pleasant evening out, so I changed the subject. But he did add that you seem to choose your enemies as carelessly as you chose your friends. After that we moved on to pleasant topics."

The Hon. Jule! The blue-blood ghoul! It had to

be Jule. The chinless bastard hadn't dared make a
formal complaint with Mrs. Throgmorton's charms
displayed to all and sundry on the counterpane.
But he'd pick up the phone, have a word with
Prince (whom he would remember from the Golden
Calf). *Off the record, Sergeant, old chappie. Thought
you ought to know, don't you know?* Twat! And for
all I know he's had a quiet word with the Director
of Education, the East Midlands Gas Board, and
my credit tailor.

But Prince was the worst. He remembered the
blue Cortina. Could this be the police keeping an
eye on him? Though, if it were, why should Prince
give this warning through Maggie? A Machiavel-
lian stimulus to action perhaps?

Suddenly a flash of joy lit up Joe's mental gloom.
If the police were showing an interest, surely this
would make a cancellation of the raid absolutely
certain!

Something of his lightening of heart must have
shown in his eyes, for Maggie, who had looked as
if she might soften again in the face of an unbur-
dening of woes, turned to leave.

He put out his hand and held her arm. The
contact reminded him that in his school-based sexual fantasies the English store-room was nearly
always the favoured location for the big scene. In
practical terms (and his fantasies were never entirely without hope) it was the only place in the
building where he could hope to be alone and
unobserved with a woman.

Play it cool, Askern, he warned himself.

"Thank Maurice, Sergeant Prince," he said.

It was the right formula.

"What's it all about, Joe?" she said turning to
him, all big worried eyes, soft moist lips and splen-
did ready-for-mothering bosom.

Every emotional atom in him cried *tell*! *tell*! But his mind knew it was quite impossible. The least he could do was make sure that others were in no way involved in his predicament, until he was sure it was no longer a predicament. Especially not people like Maggie. If he was going to confess all, Sergeant Prince was the man. That would be purposeful. It would mean he had plumped for law and order at the expense of personal safety. Whereas to tell Maggie would mean he had chosen the comfort of the confessional at the expense of making someone he was fond of as much an accessory as himself.

"Nothing," he said. "A misunderstanding. And I'm big enough to choose my own friends."

She shrugged and left. He watched her go. She was as lovely in retreat as she was face-on. A tremor compounded of affection and pure lust ran through his body. It would be nice to have a wife like Maggie.

Nice. But unlikely. Most unlikely. Still, he couldn't really see her as a copper's wife either. Even less as a convict's. Convict. The word, knell-like, tolled him back to all his woes.

By the time Friday arrived he was feeling optimistic again. He had heard nothing. It must be off. In any case, why was he so bothered? You could make out a good historical case for plundering Averingerett of every last treasure it contained. The Trevigores themselves had little claim on his affection. The Hons. Jule and Helen seemed a revolting pair of upper-class weirdos, while Lord Trevigore, from what he had read of his contributions in the Upper Chamber, sounded like an Anglican Ku-Klux-Clansman.

It would almost be a pity if nothing came of the plan.

Halfway through the day he was further cheered by the appearance of Miss Onions, flushed with tremendous indignation. She had been seen from time to time visiting the school in the evening. Questions about the Chubb trial were always met by an indignant refusal to answer on the grounds of civic duty. But she had exuded a smug confidence that things were going as she had foreseen, which boded ill for Chubb. So it had come as a thunderbolt shock to her when at the close of the prosecution's case, the judge had directed the jury to bring in a verdict of *not guilty* without letting matters go any further.

"A travesty of justice!" she cried. "He was clearly guilty!" Joe found himself exchanging smiles with Maggie, which also improved things considerably.

"Poor old Onions!" he said to her. "And lucky old Chubb!"

"Yes," she said, a slight frown puckering her exquisitely smooth brow. "I don't think Maurice will be very pleased either."

The mention of Sergeant Prince wasn't very encouraging, but the hint that Maggie didn't see eye to eye with him on matters criminal more than compensated.

"Will you go out with me again, Maggie?" he asked on an impulse.

She eyed him quizzically.

"I might do, Joe. Ask me again some time."

Which wasn't bad in the circumstances.

On Saturday, the bubble burst. When the phone rang and Jim's voice said, "Seven-thirty. Don't be late," he knew without asking that the raid was on again.

When he arrived at the meeting it seemed as if

everything had been arranged and the discussion was now purely about remuneration.

Killer and Third Man, it appeared, were on a fixed fee and reckoned that lions were worth a couple of hundred more. The other three were on percentages and Bertie wanted to adjust these in his favour, the strength of his position being his function in the marketing. Cess was not pleased but knew he was in a corner.

"Hello, lad," he said, acknowledging Joe's arrival ten minutes after it had happened. "Take a look at that."

That was a list, compiled by Bertie with expert advice, of particular items his buyers had asked for and for which a price had been agreed. This ran at between fifty and sixty per cent of their market value where this was known. The grand total was breath-taking.

"You check that, Joe," said Cess grimly, with a hard stare at Bertie. "See we're not being fiddled. There's some dishonest folk about."

"It's on then, is it?" asked Joe hopelessly.

"Bloody right it is!" said Cess. "New date, four weeks on Saturday."

"That'll be the first weekend the lions' park will be opened to the public," said Joe.

Cess laughed.

"So what? We're not letting a few lions bother us!" he said, rubbing his hands together as though eager to take on the entire animal kingdom in personal combat. Joe wondered what had happened to make the burglary feasible once more. He held out the list.

"That seems OK."

Cess stopped laughing.

"You check it, lad. Carefully. Bit by bit. I want to know everything there is to know about those items. It's important. Then make out a list of your own. Anything else worth nicking. As long as it's easily carried and the kind of stuff people buy. Remember now, whatever's on your list you get five per cent of what we flog it for. So choose well."

He paused, but Joe had the feeling there was still something to come.

"Five per cent?" he said.

"That's right. And three thousand anyway, basic. That's fair, eh," Cess said jovially.

"Three thousand?" said Joe puzzled.

"Aye. Three grand," said Cess defensively. "It's what we can afford, Joe. There's a lot of overheads in a business like this."

"Pounds?" said Joe amazed. "You're going to pay me three thousand pounds?"

"That's right."

"But why? Look, Cess, you've got me by the short hairs. All right. So I'll give you what information I can about Averingerett. But more than that, I don't want to be involved. I mean, if anyone pays me three thousand pounds, then that's for real work, isn't it? That's real involvement!"

He paused and looked defiantly around. Bertie lit a cheroot and coughed phlegmily.

"You haven't told him, Cess?" he said.

"Not yet," said Cess, just a trifle uneasily. "I still don't see . . ."

"You tell him. It makes sense. Your new scheme sounds good, but I want all the insurance I can get. You tell him."

"Tell me what?" asked Joe with growing unease. "What is there to tell me? You ask me about the house. I'll tell you all I know. That's your deal. What else is there to it?"

All the uncertainty left Cess's face.

"There's just a bit more, Joe. So listen carefully. I'll say it once. There's no point in arguing. With our new plan, speed is of the essence. We need someone who knows his way around so there's no delay in getting the business done. Bertie's very keen on the idea, and Bertie's the big man."

A note of irony had come into his voice for a moment, but Joe was not concerned with irony.

"What idea?" he demanded, an awful suspicion hardening in his mind.

"You've been promoted, lad," said Cess. "That's why you're worth three thou. You're not just adviser any more. You're coming with us on the job!"

PART TWO

*I do not know a pleasure more affecting
than to range at will over the deserted
aparments of some fine old family mansion.*
Charles Lamb

CHAPTER I

The blood pounded desperately through Joe's veins, his sight was misted, there was a roaring in his ears and his back was racked with a thin edge of pain. He knew he could not stand much more of this.

"Oh," he cried. "Oh! Oh! Ohhh!"

And "Ohhhhh!" sighed Alice.

She was really very good. In fact superb. All Joe's former notions about doing her a favour had proved a dreadful misreading of the situation. She was eager, yes; enthusiastically receptive. But she gave a good guinea for every poundsworth she received.

After all his conscious plans both for avoiding and for receiving her advances, the actual event had taken place with an unforeseeable casualness. In his own case Joe put it down to his new sense of the transience of life, rather like wartime pilots who knew their next sortie might be their last. Three weeks had passed since the last meeting with Cess. His efforts to withdraw from active participation in the robbery had failed miserably. He had taken Cess to one side, in itself a tribute to the depth of his feelings, and pleaded with him. But the ginger man had affected to take this as an effort to get more money.

"I'm not interested in money!" protested Joe. "I don't want any money."

"Piss off," said Cess, amused. "Everyone wants money. You'll get done like the rest of us if we're caught. Before or after. I know you a bit better now, Joe. You're a realist. You'll take your cut."

Reluctantly, even through his fears, Joe had to admit the diagnosis was not altogether inaccurate.

"How much of the last lot have you got left?" asked Cess, pressing home his advantage. "Precious little. Right?"

"Wrong," said Joe gloomily. "Bugger all."

Cess laughed triumphantly.

"Look, Joe," he said, confidentially. "I'd rather you didn't come along. Lord Jim's doubtful, but Bertie's got this thing about it. So set your mind to it."

"But how are you going to get in?" demanded Joe. "It's almost impossible!"

"Never you mind about that," said Cess smugly. He peeled a few fivers off a roll.

"You push off now, lad. Work on those lists. Here, take these. Enjoy yourself, but don't make a splash."

"Suddenly Joe remembered Sergeant Prince's interest and quickly he related what Maggie had told him, mentioning the blue Cortina, and adding a few extra touches to make it sound really bad.

"I thought I should let you know I might be under surveillance," he finished in his best sincerely worried voice.

Cess had roared with laughter.

"Oh, I like you, Joe, lad! Watching you! Who the hell's going to waste time watching *you*! Haven't you heard? There's a police shortage? The buggers don't have enough men to watch *me* and they know for certain I'm a criminal. Bloody delusions of grandeur, that's your trouble. Under surveillance!"

Curiously Joe had felt so hurt by this diminution of his criminal status that his mind had been partly diverted from its concern at his recent promotion in the hierarchy.

The routine of school life had helped to distance even further his new involvement, though a couple of visits from Lord Jim had ensured it didn't slip too far out of mind. Jim had been concerned to pick his brains as cleanly as possible of everything he knew about the electrical system in operation in the house, and Joe, conscious now of his own survival needs, co-operated as fully as possible, peering through technical journals in an effort to identify the type of alarm console in use at Averingerett, and answering questions whose significance often entirely escaped him. It was surprising how much he knew. Somehow he had picked up the information that a new sprinkler anti-fire system had been installed throughout the house. And that something called graphite cushions were being used somewhere.

Lord Jim reacted unemotionally to all information; but a curious kind of rapport was reached between them. Alice had twice run into the little squat man again as Joe was letting him out and regarded him with a fearful fascination which Joe thought he recognized.

Perhaps it was the feeling that he shared something with the girl; more probably it was the fact that Maggie, though on the surface as easy with him as of old, still refused to let him take her out; but whatever the cause, it had seemed perfectly right and proper to kiss Alice passionately when he bumped into her on the front doorstep one night.

He had been on his way for a fish-and-chip supper. He dined two hours later on chicken paté and chocolate mousse. Followed by coffee. With another two-hour gap between the mousse and the coffee.

It was a revelation to him. He only hoped it hadn't been a disappointment to Alice.

"Why didn't you ever marry?" he asked as he sipped his coffee.

"What makes you think I didn't?" she answered, enigmatically.

He considered the question a moment. True. It seemed unlikely that a woman of Alice's talents would go unasked. Though he had been happy enough to ignore her for long enough. Not any more though.

Thoughts of Maggie gently nudged his mind and were reluctant to be pushed away. Somehow, despite the last four hours for which he was most grateful, Maggie still seemed more *marriable*. Not that there was much chance.

"Are you then?" he asked.

"Yes," she said. "For the moment. We didn't suit."

"Oh."

"He was short of . . . stamina, I suppose."

"Oh," said Joe again, feeling uneasily short of stamina himself. But no more demands seemed in the immediate offing.

"That friend of yours. Jim? Does he teach?"

"Oh yes." Joe laughed. "In a way."

"He seems . . . interesting."

"He's certainly that," replied Joe.

Shortly afterwards he made his way back to his own flat, driven partly by fatigue but also by a reluctance to answer any more questions about Lord Jim. It would have been too easy in the comfortable half-awakening of a shared bed to confide more than a good criminal should.

When he glanced out of his window, smiling at

the picture of himself as the master criminal, he was jerked awake by the sight of the blue Cortina parked directly opposite the house. Suddenly angry, he grabbed his dressing-gown round his shoulders, raced back down the stairs and flung open the front door just in time to see the Cortina's tail-lights disappearing round the corner. He watched them go, his anger subsiding to a cold unease. Who the hell was it? The police? Cess even? And why either?

They're not very good at it anyway, he tried to reassure himself. Not very successfully.

I only know the one I've seen, his thoughts went on. And God knows how long it was before I spotted him.

He shivered, realized it wasn't just his fear that made him cold, and quickly closed the door.

Behind him stood Alice.

"What's the matter?" she asked.

"Nothing," said Joe. "Just a car. I thought it was in some kind of trouble, but it's gone now."

"I see," said Alice. She had put on a plain cotton nightdress with no pretensions to seductiveness, but there was something very alluring about it nonetheless. She went back into her flat.

"Another coffee?" she asked through the half-open door.

Joe realized he felt wide awake. At least an hour's sleepless worrying lay in store for him upstairs.

"All right," he said, closing her door behind him.

"God, you look shattered!" said Vernon the next morning. "What've you been up to? Trying to break the world record?"

"Insomnia," said Joe.

"I bet. Hey, what about a game next Saturday? You look as if you could do with some fresh air?"

Next Saturday! How wonderful to be able to talk of next Saturday as though the world did not end there.

"Sorry," said Joe. "I can't. I'm booked up."

"Aha! A woman!"

"No," said Joe vehemently, suddenly aware that Maggie was within earshot.

"Then if it's not a woman, it must be that bloody house of yours. They're the only two things which interfere with your golf. Well?"

"You should have been a detective," said Joe, thinking that at least he could be permitted some tragic irony. They might all remember this when he was languishing in jail. "Yes, I'm off to Averingerett. It's about time I finished this thesis."

He waved a cardboard wallet in the air and a couple of loose sheets of paper fell out. Maggie picked them up and glanced down at them. One was the personal list which Cess had told him to make. The other was a copy of Bertie's list, with certain additional information about some items for Lord Jim's benefit. Though why he should be interested in the exact weight of things Joe could not imagine.

"You have been working hard," said Maggie, handing the papers back. She looked at Joe with new respect.

"Not really," said Joe. "Just thinking about it. You've got to get your materials together."

It was odd how guilty he felt talking to Maggie. Guilty at his absurd lies. Guilty at the memory of Alice's slender legs locking round his buttocks.

"And you're going on Saturday? You always said you'd take me some day," said Maggie, smiling magnificently at him.

Christ! She can't mean it! She's not going to

pick this moment to forgive and forget! thought Joe in a panic.

"I'm booked up on Saturday this week," Maggie went on. "But it's open on Sunday, isn't it?"

"Yes. Oh yes. It is," said Joe, his mind racing. "But I've got to go on Saturday. I've made arrangements. I know the chief steward and he lets me work in one of the private rooms. The Trevigores are away, you see, and as I say, I've made arrangements . . ."

You're gabbling, he told himself. You're talking too much. And you're not sounding convincing. She's ready to bury the hatchet, which is what you want, but this sounds like a snub. But what can I do? I might be in jail in a few days' time!

Maggie nodded, her smile merely polite now.

"I see," she said. "What a pity. Another time."

She turned away.

You're a fool! Joe told himself. For all you know, you'll wake up on Sunday morning a free man with three thousand quid in your pocket. A man could get married on that. You could pretend it was a dowry or something. Tell mam it's an old Cohen custom; that might calm her down a bit!

"Maggie," he said, more loudly than he intended. At the same time he caught her arm and turned her body towards him. Everyone else in the staff-room watched the scene with undisguised interest.

"Yes?" she said.

"I do have to go on Saturday," he said, "but that's no reason why I shouldn't go again on Sunday. Or any other day. I would love to take you. Nothing would please me more."

Maggie glanced round at her colleagues.

"Well, that's all right then," she said. But the warmth of her tone belied the casualness of her words. The bell sounded the start of morning school and there was a general movement to the door. Maggie detached herself gently from Joe's grip.

"See you later," she said, squeezing his hand.

While the prospect of a full reconciliation with Maggie was a source of great comfort to Joe, he was very conscious now that the nightmare of the plan to enter Averingerett was fast approaching reality. Maggie would probably have gone out with him immediately, he felt sure. She wasn't the kind to play hard to get without good reason. But some outmoded sense of chivalry made him reluctant to start things going again until Saturday was over. After that, all being well, Sergeant Prince would have a fight on his hands.

In any case, he was expecting daily to be summoned for the final briefing and he didn't want to start his rehabilitation with Maggie by breaking a date.

And he knew that, if Cess called, he would certainly break the date.

The briefing took place on the Friday night and was something of an anti-climax. Lord Jim called just as he was about to go into Alice's for a bite of supper. He had started avoiding her again in the face of his new committal to Maggie; but he had decided that, if he owed it to Maggie to postpone their reconciliation in case he was jailed, he owed it to himself to take a long farewell of Alice for the very same reason.

"Smells nice," said Jim. "Cess'd like a word."

"Sorry," said Joe to Alice and to Jim, "I'll drive myself."

"Suit yourself," said Lord Jim.

Joe left him standing in the hall and went to get his car.

To his surprise when he arrived at the pub, Cess

met him in the bar. None of the others was in sight.

"Hello, Joe," said the ginger man. "You needn't order. This won't take but a minute. You know the oak-tree junction on the main road seven miles this side of Averingerett?"

"Yes."

"There's an unclassified road off to the left about two hundred yards before you reach it. There's a lay-by about fifty yards up there, not so much a lay-by, more a bit of hard-standing at the road side. You be there at two-thirty tomorrow. Got that?"

"Yes," said Joe surprised. "Two-thirty? In the morning?"

Cess rolled his eyes.

"Jesus," he said. "No. The afternoon. We're going to bloody Averingerett, aren't we? And they shut the gates at six, don't they?"

"Yes," said Joe. "How do we get out?"

"You let me worry. Just you be there on time. Look for a Bedford van. Cheerio."

Bewildered, Joe headed for the door. Just coming in was Cynthia.

"Hello, Joe," she said.

"Hello, Cyn."

"Look after yourself, eh?"

Touched, he nodded wordlessly and stood by to let her past.

"And if there's any trouble," she murmured, "don't start swinging punches. You're not cut out for it. Just run like hell."

"I promise," he said fervently.

Nice girl, he thought out in the street. Who's more to be pitied—her or Mrs. Carter? Either. Both. All of us!

The real briefing, he worked out with some bitterness, must have taken place days earlier. Only he had been kept in the dark till the last minute, and, even then, just given a rendezvous place and time.

Stuff them all! he thought, driving home, warmed by the thought of the soldier's farewell there was going to be plenty of time for after all.

But when he knocked at Alice's door there was no reply. She can't have gone out, he thought and tried again. Still nothing. Perhaps there was something wrong. He started banging with both fists and was so carried away by his own percussion rhythms that when the door was suddenly pulled open he almost smashed his fist into Lord Jim's face.

"Oh it's you," grunted the little man. He was wearing only his trousers. His face was flushed and his magnificently muscled torso gleamed with perspiration. He looked as if he had just come last in a fell race.

The two men faced each other unspeaking for a moment.

"I was just having your supper," said Jim finally.

"Jim," called Alice's voice plaintively.

"Steak pie," added Jim. "There's plenty."

There was almost a note of appeal in his voice.

"Jim!" called Alice again, more insistently.

Joe stepped back from the door.

"No. No thanks. You finish it," he said. "But don't bite off more than you can chew."

It wasn't a bad line. But it was hardly compensation for the soldier's farewell. Thoughts of the battle ahead crowded in on him as he wearily made his way upstairs to a cold supper and a lonely bed.

He lay awake for a long time, listening again

and again to Garland singing "Somewhere Over The Rainbow," till Vardon jumped up beside him and, somewhat comforted, he drifted into a sleep which God (who is good to sinners) swept clean of the threatened nightmares and filled instead with the warm, white, lucent, million-pleasured breasts of Maisie Uppadine.

CHAPTER II

Mindful of Cess's warning, he was ready in plenty of time the next day. The phone rang as he was on the point of leaving the flat. It was Cess.

"I'm just off," Joe said.

"No hurry, Joe" said Cess. "You don't want to get there early. It's bad for the nerves, hanging about. Everthing OK?"

"Yes."

"Got everything you need?"

"Yes."

"Right then. See you later."

"Was that all you wanted?" asked Joe angrily.

"Don't be so touchy, lad," said Cess, aggrieved. "I was just checking that you were all right. A friendly word can help a lot at a time like this."

Surprisingly, Joe found himself believing him. "Sorry," he said. "It was a kind thought. I'll see you soon."

Quickly he checked round the flat once more. It wouldn't be helpful to leave a tap running at a time like this and have everyone out looking for him. Vardon watched him impatiently, obviously bent on getting back into Joe's bed the minute he left.

The thought flashed through Joe's mind that if things went wrong, this might be the last time he saw the flat for a long time. Did they let you home from the nick to collect your gear? More likely a gaggle of ham-fisted coppers would come and turn everything over. He thought of them pulling open drawers, running their fingers through his special-occasion way-out underwear, reading his private letters, emptying the box in which he kept his emergency supply of contraceptives. Vardon would be furious. He hoped some of them liked cats.

"Cheerio, you fat pig," he said. Vardon yawned disdainfully. It was time to go.

It took two turns of the key to get the VW started. An omen? Three black birds settled on a chimney stack at the end of the street. He searched in his memories of folklore to find a significance for them, but could only come up with the "twa corbies" of the ballad. That was bad enough. He glanced up at them as he approached the main-road junction and almost collided with a dark-green Hillman which was cutting the corner rather fine. Instinctively he stamped on the brake and was thrown forward against the steering wheel. The Hillman halted also, almost alongside.

Joe wound down the window.

"You stupid bastard!" he yelled at the man dimly visible behind the dusty glass. The woman passenger leaned across and opened the door. It was Maggie.

"Hi!" she said with a bright smile. "You should look where you're going."

Beside her, smiling too, was Sergeant Prince looking very sporty in a flowered T-shirt and orange slacks.

"No harm done anyway," Maggie went on. "I'm glad we caught you. Just off to Averingerett, are you? Well, do you have room for a small passenger and a large picnic-basket?"

"My idea," said Prince. "I've been summoned for duty. No rest for the anti-wicked. It seemed a shame to waste a nice day and a picnic, so I told her to find herself another poor bachelor."

"And I knew you were off to do the stately homes bit again, so here I am," said Maggie, almost defiantly.

There had to be an excuse. *I've changed my mind. I'm not going.* But she might go by herself and see him there. *I've arranged to take somebody else.* Better, but the same objection.

In any case, any refusal would be a humiliation for her. He might as well say *I don't take pig's leftovers* and drive on.

Whatever he did, he couldn't take her. It was out of the question. Absolutely.

"Careful with the basket. There's a bottle of hock in a plastic bag filled with ice," said Maggie as she climbed in beside him. "Thanks for the lift, Maurice. Don't accept any dud alibis."

"Have fun," said Prince, letting in the clutch. "Take care of her."

A warning? wondered Joe, his brain racing madly. Prince was on to him. Maggie was a plant. At the first sign of anything odd, she'd be on the phone in a flash.

"Right, Joseph," she said leaning back in her seat, "you may drive me to Lord Trevigore's."

He had to return her smile. No, it was impossible; there was no subterfuge here. In fact the whole scene had been stamped with Maggie's personal brand of complete honesty. Prince wasn't for her, not as a serious long-term proposition. So she'd make this quite clear, as nicely as possible. While he, Joe, had been weighed in the balance and found wanted. It sounded cold-blooded, but he knew it wasn't like that. If anything, it was very flattering. But what the hell was he going to do?

He had stalled the engine. When he turned the key to start it again, the sudden noise startled the three birds and they rose laboriously into the air on ragged wings, croaking harshly.

"I've got the message," muttered Joe and turned the car carefully into the main road.

They didn't speak for the next ten minutes until the buildings began to thin out and the soft summer greenery to fill in.

"You don't mind, do you, Joe?" asked Maggie suddenly.

"Of course not," croaked Joe, his sincerity at one level clashing harshly with his insincerity at another.

"Good," she said happily. "When Maurice got this call, I wasn't really disappointed, just a bit at first, but then I suddenly thought, what I'd really like to do is go to Averingerett with Joe. You did say you'd take me."

"Yes. Did I? It's different now," said Joe as though she might say *Well, in that case, drop me here. I'll go home.*

"How?"

"They've got lions." Bloody lions! If it wasn't for the stupid damned lions he mightn't be here now, on his way to a house-breaking.

"Of course they have. Super! Lions and an expert guide!"

She settled back again, radiating complete animal content.

Oh God! thought Joe. If only this was another day, another place! What shall I do? She had to be got rid of. He couldn't miss the rendezvous. And certainly he couldn't turn up at the house with her *and* the car. Either would be disastrous. Both unforgivable.

Surreptitiously he glanced at his watch. Still a bit of time in hand. Get rid of her, get rid of her!

The thought was running in panic round his mind. But how? without being obvious. How?

Make *her* suggest it; make her *want* to go.

Be nasty? Say something snide about Prince? Start a quarrel *somehow*.

It was in a flash. There was one area in which they had never been able to reach full agreement. They could fall out here and she wouldn't be able to hold it against him.

Two minutes later he turned into a side-road and then turned again and bumped along a hawthorn-hedged lane for ten or fifteen yards before stopping the car.

She looked at him, mildly surprised.

"Breath of air," he said, glancing at his watch again.

"All right," she said.

They walked hand in hand a little further down the lane, till they reached a gate which overlooked a field of young barley.

"Over we go," said Joe. He let his hand rest boldly on her thigh as he helped her over. There was no time for subtlety. In fact the more blatant he was, the sooner she would reject his advances.

He took her in his arms and kissed her as soon as they got into the field, then sank to the ground, pulling her down after him.

There was no resistance, just a self-containment which boded well. She was poised for action, he felt.

He ignored the shallows where his advances had usually foundered in the past and sought an instant rebuff by pulling her skirt roughly up round her behind. Still nothing. He stuck his thumbs inside her pants and began dragging them down the swooningly smooth slopes of her thighs. As they passed over her knees she drew his head down to hers and kissed him passionately. He gasped for breath beneath the violence of her onslaught, and his heart sank as he felt her legs kicking the pants over her ankles. Then one hand came down to the buckle of his belt. And he knew he was lost.

The next ten minutes were the most humiliating of his life. His motives for being there, his awareness of the night ahead, his sense of the omnipresence of Cess and Lord Jim, all came between him and the business in hand. His usually over-eager flesh failed miserably, refusing to respond to even the most intimate ministration from Maggie. Finally they lay apart and he gazed up at the bright blue sky whose gaiety now seemed to have an edge of cruelty and even the jolly yellow sun seemed to be mocking him.

"Did I do something wrong?" she asked.

"No. Oh no. Nothing. Nothing."

She hesitated a moment.

"Is there something that helps? I mean, should I be wearing stockings? Or black lace? Something like that. I read somewhere that . . ."

"No! Nothing like that. It's nothing like that. Really."

He stood and began dressing himself. Slowly she followed suit. It was like the setting of the sun.

Back in the car, he had recovered sufficiently to glance at his watch again. Time was short. Not that this first rendezvous was all that important. But he had to get there; and without Maggie.

He began to back the car down the lane. As he slowed down at the entrance to the road, he saw his salvation slowly breasting a rise about two furlongs away. A bus.

He stopped the car, jumped out and hurried round to Maggie's door.

She stared at him incredulously.

"Again?" she asked. He ignored her.

"Maggie," he said, "I'm sorry about everything. Please, do you mind? I'd like to be alone. To think. It means a lot. To a man. Could you, would you, go back to town by yourself? On the bus?"

Now her incredulity was anything but slight.

"What?" she cried.

"Maggie, please!" The bus was approaching fast. The panic in his voice must have sounded like a cry from a wounded spirit, for she softened immediately.

"If that's what you want, Joe."

He turned away with unseemly haste and ran across the road, waving at the bus. As it slowed down, Maggie came up behind him and took his hand. He turned. Her face was full of concern.

"Are you sure you're all right, love?"

"Yes. Yes. Sure. Goodbye."

He pushed her firmly up the steps. Oddly enough the purely functional contact with her body through her cardigan did what all the wiles of nudity had been unable to, and as he waved at the retreating bus he felt himself roused ready for action.

"Damn! damn! damn!" he cried aloud. Why did it have to be today? Why couldn't she have been as resolute against the final attack as she had always been in the past? And why had all the background scenery—sunshine, flowers, birdsong, etc. etc. —been so perfect for such a shoddy performance? Up against a wall, in a bus-shelter, in the park even, it might hardly have mattered. You could forget it, blame it on the drink, the Chinese food, the damp air.

But here!

"Damn!" he said.

"Where the hell have you been?" said Cess.

"For Christ's sake, stop talking to me like the office boy!" snarled Joe. "Get this, and get it good. You need me. You need me a lot. OK? And while we're at it, I think five per cent's not enough. I want ten per cent of the extra stuff. Right?"

Cess looked at him in amazement. Lord Jim flexed his broad back-muscles significantly. Bertie laughed out loud while Killer and Third Man stayed dough-faced and drew on their hand-rolled cigarettes.

What have I said? thought Joe, the anger and frustration which had built up during the rest of his drive evaporating in the heat of his own folly. But Cess when he spoke was conciliatory.

"All right, Joe. Don't get so het up. We'll talk about it later. I know how important you are. We all do, believe me. Right, Jim?"

"Yeah," said Jim.

"I was only five minutes late," said Joe, sullenly. "It doesn't matter."

"Not now it doesn't. But later, we've got to be on the ball. So we might as well try to start right."

They were standing round a Volkswagen minibus which was parked in a lay-by overhung by trees so that they were all shiftingly dappled by sunlight. Joe had nearly missed them as he was looking for a Bedford van.

"Sod who owned it's gone off for the weekend," explained Cess sourly. "So we had to make do with this kraut thing."

He kicked a tyre mistrustingly and shot a nasty glance at Joe's beetle.

"Right, Joe. Hop aboard. Let's get going."

"Will my car be all right here?" wondered Joe.

"What do you want. A bleeding lock-up? You've got insurance, haven't you? Leave your wallet and stuff in it. Anything that might identify you. And hide your key somewhere."

Unhappily Joe obeyed and clambered into the mini-bus. Lord Jim got into the driving-seat with Cess beside him. Bertie and Third Man joined Joe in the back where a couple of large cardboard boxes lay on the floor.

"Our gear," explained Bertie, catching Joe's puzzled glance.

Killer slammed the door and made his way to a Vauxhall estate-wagon farther along the lay-by.

"Why's he not coming?" asked Joe.

"We need someone on the outside, don't we?" said Bertie amiably. "To protect our rear."

The thought of relying on Killer for anything as important as their escape route made Joe relapse into a dark melancholia for the rest of the trip.

They met the queue of traffic making its way to Averingerett a good half-mile from the house. Lord Jim tried jumping the queue, cutting in sharply in front of a bus, which blew an angry horn.

"Watch it!" said Cess warningly.

The hold-up was obviously at the bridge where entrance money was collected, or rather at the second gate some fifty yards on the other side of the bridge where the park proper began. A dozen cars at a time were let through, then the barrier came down again till there was sufficient space on the park-road to take the next dozen. Meanwhile the bridge barrier went up, permitting the next twelve cars to fill the space between the two gates, which were never open simultaneously. Men in Sanders-of-the-River gear collected the money, and there were four, two on each gate, who carried heavy rifles and stood looking keenly into the park.

The precautions, Joe suspected, were as much for show as necessity. The particular white hunter who took their money had spectacles like a Victorian sweet-shop window and his long hair made his bush-hat seem more appropriate to Ascot than a big-game park.

Behind all this almost irreverent and pantomimic activity at the bridge, the great house lay imperturbable in its strength and beauty. Joe's heart turned over as he looked at it. He could never enter it as an owner but tonight at least he would take by force that which others had so casually acquired.

Like Tarquin and Lucrece, he thought, and laughed at his own absurdity. The barrier rose ahead and the mini-bus rolled slowly forward into the Great Park.

Eighty yards ahead the road forked, the great majority of cars carrying straight on to make the full encirclement of the park leading eventually to the exit over the south bridge. Those wishing to visit the house as well as see the lions forked right here and passed through another well-manned gate into the car-park by the stables.

As they approached this gate Cess turned round and began to talk.

"Right, Joe, lad," he said, "here's the plan."

He'll tell me now, thought Joe. He thinks we're committed.

It was a dreadful plan. He had expected something incredibly subtle, too clever for the non-professional mind to conceive. Instead he was told they were going to stay behind after closing time. Cess even looked as if he expected him to be impressed.

"In the house?" he demanded incredulously. "You can't stay in the house! No one can. They go through it with a finetooth comb every night!"

"No. Not in the house," said Cess scornfully. "In the garden."

Joe rolled his eyes.

"In the grotto," explained Bertie, watching his reaction with flattering anxiety. "How's that grab you?"

Joe considered. He had to admit the grotto might work. In fact, if he had been consulted, as he bloody well should have been as the Averingerett expert, the caves of the Blue Grotto were exactly what he would have recommended.

"The grotto, eh?" he said coldly. "I suppose that might work. But what the hell happens then? How are we going to get into the house without sounding the alarm?"

New objections were rushing to offer themselves. He peered down at the sellotape-sealed cardboard boxes.

"This stuff, you can't lug these around with you! And the van, what's going to happen to the van? And how are we going to get out through the park?"

"Bloody amateurs!" groaned Cess.

Bertie patted his shoulder sympathetically.

"All taken care of, Joe boy! At least," he said, eyeing Cess thoughtfully, "we've been given big assurances it's all taken care of."

Cess swung round again, his teeth showing in a Geronimo snarl.

"Careful!" said Lord Jim. "We're here!"

They pulled into the crowded car-park and found a spot next to the stables' wall. To Joe it seemed that the car-park attendants stared curiously at this vanload of five ill-assorted men.

Perhaps they'll think we're the Gay Liberation Front on a day outing, he told himself hopefully.

"What happens now?" he asked as Lord Jim pulled open his door.

"Now? Now we take a walk around. Enjoy the gardens. Look at the treasures. Get the feel of the place. Have a cup of tea. Act like the rest of these mugs."

Cess jerked his head scornfully at the line of people, shirt-sleeved and summer-frocked against the hot sun, making their way slowly under the stable arch.

"Be inconspicuous. We split up now. Then about half past five, make your way casually up to the Blue Grotto. And don't leave it too late. You know your way there, do you, Joe?" Ironically.

"You can't miss it," said Joe. "Past the sign saying *Dangerous, do not Pass this sign.*"

No one laughed.

"And have a piddle before you come to the grotto," said Cess. "It's a long wait till dark."

Now they all laughed, even Joe. Cess liked to be appreciated.

"Off you go, Joe," said Cess, almost kindly. "We don't know each other if we meet. But don't worry. Lord Jim'll stick close."

With this comforting thought in his mind, Joe plunged into the crowd of people making their way under the arch, over which the cracked bell of the invisible clock struck three.

Three hours till closing time.

The rooms were unpleasantly crowded compared with last time, and the Averingerett policy of letting people make their way round at their own speed was in danger of bringing all movement to a halt. For the first time the beauties of the old house began to pall and Joe used his shoulder ruthlessly to force a passage through the crowds. Even so, he found his mind automatically checking that all was as it should be, everything in its accustomed place. Criminal conditioning! he thought ruefully, cutting between an ugly small boy and his mother. The boy set up a terrible howl and momentarily conscience-stricken, Joe turned to re-unite them. From behind a hand gripped him firmly by the shoulder and his criminal conditioning threw up a sweat of sheer terror all over his body.

"Here again, Joe?" said Jock Laidlaw.

"Christ, Jock!" said Joe, shaking. "Jesus Christ!"

"You're a glutton for punishment," said Jock lifting two bottles of Guinness out of the cupboard in his room. The thick stone walls of the stables ensured it was always cool in here and, while Joe would rather have avoided his old friend today, it was a relief to get out of the heat and the crowds.

"All alone, are you?" continued Jock. "No kids? Or a girl?"

"No," said Joe sadly.

"Pity," said Jock. "It's time you got married and settled down."

"That's great advice coming from an old bachelor like you!"

"Maybe so," said Jock, unrepentant. "Me, I'm married to my job so to speak. You're not, Joe, if I'm not mistaken. It wouldn't break your heart if you never saw another classroom in your life, eh? But me, I love looking after this place."

He looked lovingly around, as if his eyes were seeing beyond the solid walls of the room into the great chambers and the rich gardens of Averingerett.

"Man, I'll be happy here till I die. You though, Joe, you need a woman."

No, thought Joe. Not a woman. I need my head examined. I need to be beaten through the streets with rods of iron. If anything goes wrong tonight, it's not just me that will be caught and punished. Everyone knows I'm a mate of Jock's. This could lash back at him, maybe lose him his job. I haven't the right.

He downed his drink and stood up, his face set with resolution. Cess had to be told immediately. Jock looked surprised.

"What's your hurry, laddie? Have another."

"No thanks. I've got to be pushing on."

"Suit yourself." Laidlaw glanced at his watch. "I'll walk a-ways with you."

He pushed open the door of the control-room as they passed. A man was sitting at the console monitoring walkie-talkie messages from the park-wardens and gate-keepers.

"All well?"

"Fine, Mr. Laidlaw. Couple of fools leaning out of windows to take photographs, but we got to them before any damage was done."

"Funny things, people," said Jock as they moved on. "They'll look twice before crossing the road but they don't really worry about dangers they don't understand."

"Then the lions are really wild?"

Jock shot him an ironically amused glance.

"You believe me, Joe. Don't find out the hard way."

They stopped outside the entrance hall.

"I'll leave you to fight your way through the mob," said the steward. "I'm off to check that his lordship's rooms are in order."

"Trevigore?" said Joe. "But I thought that lot had all left for fresh woods and pastures new?"

"Aye, they did. But they'll be back tonight. It's his lordship's birthday and they're having a wee bittie of a party. It's a damn nuisance." He spoke with grave disapproval. His love of the house was in no way linked to a love of the Trevigore family. Indeed Joe often felt he regarded them as bothersome intruders. And certainly the thought of frivolous celebrations disturbing the peace of Averingerett would give him great offence.

But the causes of the streak of Puritanism in Jock were far from Joe's mind as he re-entered the house. So the Trevigores were back! Would this in itself be sufficient to put Cess off the job that night? Bertie was a better bet. He obviously liked his operations cut and dried. Unexpected changes of circumstance brought unprepared-for risks. Cess would be much harder to turn aside once he had gone so far.

In any case, thought Joe, the job's off. If they don't decide it, I will. I'm not putting Jock's head on the chopping-block, no matter what they do to me.

He pressed through the crowd once more, hoping for a glimpse of Cess. Or even Lord Jim whose proximity had been so threateningly promised. But there was no sign of either. The determination in his mind was now at constant war with the fear in his belly, and as the struggle grew more violent, his head began to swim and he had to lean against an alabaster pillar, sharing its support with the neanderthal bust of the seventh earl.

The door at the end of the Long Gallery seemed an uncrossable distance away and the intervening space was odoriferously packed with sweating visitors whom the heat seemed to have fused together.

The whole scene wobbled like a desert mirage on the point of disappearing. And now his ears were going too.

"Joe! Joe!" a voice seemed to be calling; sweet,

bell-like; angelic. Perhaps this was the way the end always began.

Then suddenly, violently, everything clicked back into sharp focus.

Standing in the doorway, waving her hand and calling out over the heads of the intervening throng, was Maggie. She felt his gaze lock with hers, a broad smile broke dawn-like over her face and she began to fight her way towards him.

Pushing off from the pillar with a violence that almost dislodged the seventh earl, Joe plunged back into the crowd and did not let consideration of either sex or age impede his retreat till he was out in the garden and making his way through the protection of an azalea grove towards the Blue Grotto.

CHAPTER III

How Maggie had made her way to the house he did not know. Nor was he very eager to find out. Another encounter with her now was out of the question. If her eagerness to see him had survived his recent flight, she would probably look for his car in the car-park. When that failed, there would be nothing left for her but to make her way home by whatever means she had come.

But while there was still a chance that she was wandering around the house looking for him, he did not dare venture forth again.

He wouldn't have minded so much if only it had been cool inside the caves of the grotto, but the air seemed to hang heavily and there was a musty smell which pervaded everything. He suspected it was a remnant of the days when the grotto offered the nearest thing to a public convenience in this part of the gardens. He hoped now the warning notice and two strands of barbed-wire would deter any potential users.

The Blue Grotto, so called because of the bluey-grey stone which predominated, had been created in the nineteenth century to satisfy the Romantic tastes of the sixth earl. The boulder against which Joe rested at this moment was part of the rock-fall blocking the main cave which had formerly run right through the grotto. As the gigantic rockery now formed part of the barrier separating the house gardens from the lions' park, it seemed unlikely that the passage would ever be restored.

Joe glanced at his watch. Two hours till closing time. His stomach rumbled appealingly and he had a sudden vision of Maggie's picnic-basket and the hock in the ice-filled plastic bag. They were still in his car. He wished with all his heart he were with them. Disconsolately he brought his knees up to his chest and settled down to wait, dimly recalling that this was the position in which some South American Indians arranged their dead.

He must have fallen asleep for he was awoken by a hand shaking his shoulder and Bertie's voice saying, "Give 'im a kiss and tell 'im the spell is broke."

It was Third Man doing the shaking. Joe grunted a greeting and peered at his watch. Only fifteen minutes to closing time. Cess would be here soon. He had to use the time to sow seeds of worry in Bertie's mind. The refusal absolute face to face with Cess was something he still hoped to avoid.

"Bertie," he said urgently. "I was talking to Laidlaw, the head steward. The Trevigores are here tonight. There's a party of some kind. God knows how long it'll go on for."

Bertie looked discouragingly unconcerned and Joe opened his mouth to clarify what he had just said in case there had been a misunderstanding.

"Good," said Cess approvingly from the mouth of the cave. "I told you, Bertie."

"I believed you, Cess, else I wouldn't be here, would I?" said Bertie. "You want a medal or something? For hobnobbing with the nobs?"

For a moment Cess looked offended. But Joe broke in before he could speak.

"You know? How?"

"I move in the right circles," said Cess smugly.

"Then why are we here? We can't break in while the house is occupied."

"Wrong," said Cess. "With that alarm-system, we can't break in while the house *isn't* occupied."

Why am I arguing? wondered Joe. All I've got to do is tell him that it doesn't matter whether the house is occupied or not, it's off.

Listen, Cess. This is the end of the road. I've come this far for the giggle, but enough's enough. Run along home now, there's a good little criminal. Vandalize a phone box and go to bed happy.

"No," he said aloud.

"No? No what?" asked Cess.

"No thanks," suggested Bertie.

"I can't, I mean I won't; look, it's not just me. I mean . . ."

They were all looking at him curiously.

"What are you trying to say, lad?" asked Cess, his Indian-brave look very much in evidence.

"I've changed my mind!" he blurted out.

Bertie rolled his eyes revoltingly and muttered, "Me mother told me never to stray north of Stanmore."

Cess began to clench his fists persuasively, Third Man yawned, Joe pressed himself back against the boulder. It moved slightly, then slid a few inches as though it had been unevenly balanced on some loose stones.

"I thought we'd put all that behind us, Joe," said Cess advancing.

Despite all his efforts to stay relaxed, Joe felt himself cringing away. He tried to force himself upright, but it was as if some heavy hand lay on his shoulder pulling him down. Even when Cess stopped dead in his tracks then took a step backwards, he found he could not move. The musty smell was suddenly very strong.

He knew what it was an instant before the deep, rasping growl bubbled in his ears and, turning his head, he saw that when the boulder had moved, a gap of some nine to twelve inches had opened up. Through it, clawing curiously at his jacket shoulder, stretched a lion's paw.

His panic-stricken leap forward landed him almost in Cess's arms but the ginger man had suddenly been deposed from the number-one menace spot. As though equally startled by his sudden movement, the paw was swiftly and silently withdrawn.

"Jesus!" said Bertie.

"Jesus!" said Joe, Cess, and Third Man altogether.

"Joe!" said a new voice. "Oh, Joe!"

Fate had decided unexpected lion's paws were not enough to unstring Joe's nerves. Another assault was made on him from behind. Spinning round again, he found himself clutching a warm, gently shaking, female body, a pleasurable experience at any other time. But not now. It was Maggie.

"Jesus!" said Joe unimaginatively.

"Oh Joe!" cried Maggie.

"I found her outside," said Lord Jim. "Watching."

Cess restored himself instantly to the number-one spot.

"You told her, Joe?" he demanded threateningly.

"No! No, I didn't," replied Joe, noting with distress that for the second time in a day Maggie's beautiful breasts were heaving uninhibitedly against his chest without causing him the slightest physical disturbance.

Cess glowered at him disbelievingly. Then Maggie spoke.

"No, it was you," she said, uncertainly at first, but recovering her self-possession fast. "I followed you here from the van."

"The van?" queried Joe.

"Yes. That bus you put me on wasn't going back

to town at all. It was coming here! I nearly got off when I found out but I thought, why the hell should I? I wanted to see the house. It seemed daft not going just because ... And, anyway, you had my picnic and wine."

She looked defiantly at Joe, who essayed a small smile.

"How'd you know he was in a van?" demanded Cess.

"I saw him from the bus. You cut in on us just before the entrance." She turned back to Joe. "I've been looking for you all day, but when you disappeared in the crowd, I headed for the car-park and found the van. It seemed sensible to wait there. Then *he*, (it's Mr. Carter, isn't it? Mickey's father?) came along, fiddled about under the bonnet and had a word with one of the attendants. I heard him say he couldn't start it and could he use the telephone? There was a lot of coming and going, but finally he said something about leaving the van there overnight and getting a lift home with some friends. So I followed him. I thought he'd be going back to the house or somewhere. But he came up here to the caves. I was standing outside wondering what to do when Charles Atlas here turned up and pushed me in."

"Sorry," said Lord Jim. Real old-fashioned courtesy! thought Joe. He looks as if he means it!

"What's going on, anyway?" demanded Maggie. She looked at her watch. "It's closing time, don't you know that? What're you all doing in here like a lot of troglodytes?"

Bertie, who had spent the last few minutes feverishly pushing loose stones into the gap above the boulder, spoke for the first time.

"It's a right mess, Cess," he said gloomily. "Let's call it a day, old son, eh? Everything's against us.

Bloody lions crawling through holes, Joe-boy jittery as a drunken nun, and now Miss—Whatsit here."

"Cohen," said Maggie. "Maggie Cohen."

"No relation to Allie Cohen who's got the betting shops in Ilford?" asked Bertie with interest.

"For God's sake!" snarled Cess.

Joe looked at him with new interest. Uncertainty showed through every feature where previously little other than naked menace had ever made an impression. He glanced at his ostentatiously expensive watch, the kind which concealed the time beneath a whole complex of astronomic and atmospheric information.

He'd like to make a phone call! thought Joe. But he can't. It's too late.

"She does know your name too, Cess," said Third Man apologetically. Joe had never heard him speak before. Now he felt like embracing him as a new and unexpectedly strong ally.

"Well?" said Maggie. "Is no one going to tell me?"

"To tell the truth, Maggie," said Joe, "we're hiding here till it's dark, then we're going to break into the house and steal about a hundred thousand quid's worth of stuff. This, as you know, is Cess Carter, who's in charge. That's Bertie playing with the stones. He's the one who looks after disposal. And this is Third Man. I'm not sure of his function, or his name for that matter."

"Simon Bunce," offered Third Man, adding apologetically, "I'm just a thief."

"There! Now you've met everybody, perhaps we ought to go."

Feeling fully in command of the situation, Joe put his arm round Maggie and took a step forward.

"Hold it," said Cess. His face had returned to normal, Joe noted uneasily.

"You're going nowhere. Nothing's changed. In fact it's lucky you came when you did, Miss."

He leered suggestively at Maggie.

"You see, Sir here was beginning to have cold feet. You're quite fond of him, eh? Aye, my lad's told me about you too. Well, you wouldn't like to see him gaoled, would you?"

Maggie shook her head with less conviction than Joe would have liked. Hopefully, he put it down to mere bewilderment.

"Hear this, then. He's done enough already to get him five years as an accessory. And we've got some pictures as well. Perhaps you'd like her to see the pictures, Joe, lad?"

"No," said Joe faintly. "No."

"Right then. We're OK, Bertie, Miss here will keep quiet for Joe's sake. And Joe will join in happily for her sake. It's the perfect set-up."

"But we can't take her into the house with us," objected Bertie. "And I don't fancy her swanning around outside while I'm on the job, begging your pardon, lady."

"That's all right," said Cess triumphantly like one who has reasoned his way to the *sic probo* in a metaphysical debate. "Before we go into the house, we knock her on the head!"

They compromised in the end on binding her hands and feet, Joe's protests having been supported by both Bertie and Third Man. Even Lord Jim had shame-facedly come out against his leader. Cess had gone as far as accepting her parole that she wouldn't cause any trouble while they were all in the cave, but, as he put it, he wouldn't have trusted the

Virgin Mary to stay by herself in the cave once the men had left.

"We'll be back for you, love," promised Joe, testing the makeshift bonds for over-tightness. "I'm sorry."

He bent down to brush her cheek with his lips. Surprisingly she turned her mouth to his and he felt her tongue running round his teeth.

"This is kinky," she whispered. "Do you think we could manage it, all tied up?"

Joe looked down at her in admiration. Obviously once she decided the time had come to give her all, she didn't let up until her all was given, even in the face of miserable failures like his own that afternoon.

"Later," he said. "I must go."

"Take care," she said.

He joined the others at the entrance to the grotto. Lord Jim he noticed, slipped back, probably to make a quick check that he hadn't untied Maggie's hands.

It was a beautiful night, clear and warm. There was no moon, but the sky was so rich with stars, there scarcely seemed room for one anyway. Though it was after midnight, it had not long been full dark. Since about nine-thirty they had watched a series of cars arriving at the house, presumably for Lord Trevigore's birthday party. Many of them had turned off on to the safari road, obviously to have a look at the lions while daylight still remained.

"I hope the bastards try it when they're going home pissed," said Cess as he peered down at the road through a small pair of binoculars. "They're thick enough to get themselves chewed up."

To Joe it seemed the same thought must have occurred to Lord Trevigore. There seemed to be a full contingent of park-wardens on duty, as well as the attendants necessary to open and close the bridge and house-gates for the visitors. It still seemed the worst possible night to have chosen for the job, but Cess seemed very happy with things, so there was little to be gained from making the point again.

The last car turned up after eleven, about an hour later than the main body. The owner seemed to have a great respect for the lions as the vehicle moved at snail's-pace from the bridge to the house, and the driver experimented with both dipped and full headlights as a potential deterrent, much to Cess's amusement.

Another hour had elapsed since then and the tension had mounted steadily, for Joe at least. Three times he had apologetically retired into the azaleas.

"Try to tighten up, Joe," Bertie had whispered confidentially after the third visit. "Too much of that weakens you."

Now, weakened or not, it seemed the time had come. Cess made a small movement of his head and set off down the slope towards the house, disappearing into the darkness after only three or four steps. Bertie and Third Man followed. Joe hesitated. A large hand pressed into the smail of his back.

"Come on."

It was Lord Jim, reappeared from the cave. He sounded quite kindly, like an old schoolmaster talking to a new boy. On their way down to the car-park, Joe was glad of his company. Three or four times he would have stumbled and fallen had not his companion steadied him with massive ease.

Things became easier once they reached the level lawns which surrounded the house, though even here Joe would have walked straight through an ornamental pond if Lord Jim had not grunted a warning. They kept clear of the building with its line of brightly-lit first-floor windows in the private apartments, till they were opposite the dark stables-block and the adjoining car-park. The VW van was where they had left it, right up against the wall. Its doors were open and the other three were busy unpacking the cardboard boxes. As they approached, Joe's foot sent a stone clicking over the gravel and the three shadowy figures spun round.

"God!" said Joe in horror, wishing for the comfort of the azaleas once more. Once again, it was a comfort to feel Lord Jim's reassuring touch.

The cause of Joe's horror was their hideously flattened faces, dimly visible as he went nearer. The explanation was almost as immediate as the shock. Nylon stockings used as masks. Only the shock lasted longer.

"Right," said Cess, unmistakable despite what the dark and his mask could do. "Quick as you can into these."

These were a pair of black gym-shoes, a black sweater and a nylon stocking. Joe took them reluctantly. It was like putting on an enemy uniform when for so long you had been pretending you were just a prisoner-of-war.

"Come on!" snapped Cess. Lord Jim was already half-changed, the others fully so and sorting out some other gear. Joe took off his jacket and tossed it into the van, pleased at the thought that he had removed all his personal effects from the pockets and left them in the glove-compartment of his own car. Why the thought pleased him, he couldn't say. It would make no difference whether they were caught or not.

Suddenly he was beset by an absolute conviction that they would be caught. Nevertheless his fingers tied the laces on his gym-shoes with careful efficiency and even pulled the absurd stocking over his head.

Bertie meanwhile had produced a walkie-talkie set from one of the boxes and was fiddling with the controls. Satisfied finally, he spoke into the attached mouthpiece.

"Blue," he said. "Blue. Blue. Blue."

"Yellow," answered a tinnily distant voice almost immediately. Joe assumed it was Killer, parked over the bridge.

"Blue, out," said Bertie, nodding with satisfaction. But Yellow wasn't satisfied.

"How's things? Everything OK?"

Cess reached over and took the radio from Bertie's hands. Placing his mouth close to the mouthpiece he said in a voice brittle with cold rage, "Bloody well belt up!"

Obviously he expected no reply. It would have taken a very brave man to essay one, thought Joe. This was not a night to bend any rules that Cess had laid down.

The initial exchange, he worked out, was all that had been required. Communication established; mutual reassurance that all was going well. The more you spoke, the more chance there was of the wrong people hearing.

"Let's go," said Cess.

He, Bertie and Third Man were carrying fairly large canvas bags, not full, but not quite empty either. Lord Jim had a coil of what looked like clothes-line over his shoulder.

"Can't I carry something?" asked Joe, with old-fashioned lower-middle-class courtesy.

"You just walk without tripping over your bol-
locks," sneered Cess. "That'll be enough."

"Please yourself," muttered Joe and strode off
angrily along the side of the stables, almost immediately stubbing his toe against the foot of a but-
tress. He hopped painfully high to the air, trying
to keep his screams in.

"Christ!" said Cess whose eyes, though invisible
behind the mask, were clearly being rolled.

The others moved, silent and sure-footed, along
the side of the house. Cess himself took up the job
of mentor to Joe and urged him along with twice
as much roughness as Lord Jim had found necessary. The man was nervous, thought Joe with surprise. As long as this merely further honed rather
than blunted the fine edge of his generalship.

He still had no idea how they were to get into
the house. There must be some connection with
the party, otherwise how to explain Cess's obvious
foreknowledge? But what it could be was beyond
him. Perhaps they would merely knock at the door
and be admitted by some venerable butler?

Cabaret for his Lordship's party, he imagined Cess
saying. *Miss Sylvie and her Exotic Dancers, at your
service.*

How exotic could you get? he wondered, looking
ahead at Lord Jim, whose usual grotesqueness had
been given a new dimension by the addition of a
nylon stocking. He had pulled it down over his
face till only the foot remained, flopping rakishly
over his left ear and giving him the outline of
some bloated pixie. Suddenly he stopped and Joe
wondered fearfully if he had spoken out loud. But
the little man's attention was fixed firmly on the
upper reaches of the house.

Joe followed his gaze. They had come right along

the building to the inhabited end and now stood beneath the line of festal light on the first floor.

Perhaps he's going to sprout wings and soar aloft like Peter Pan. Or Dumbo.

Something slightly less dramatic but just as unexpected happened. A first-floor window opened and a naked man stepped out on to the sill. Joe felt himself thrown forward with tremendous force so that he crashed violently against the wall. It was Cess, of course. The others without any prompting were already hugging the side of the house as though it were the breasts of Venus herself.

Painful though the experience was, Joe could not altogether blame Cess. Unaided, he would certainly have remained on the edge of the lawn marvelling at the strange apparition above.

Next moment he was glad he hadn't. There was a reedy cacophony of well-bred laughter overhead, accompanied by the easily recognized sound of a thin jet of liquid striking the ground only a yard away.

"Dirty bastard!" snarled Cess softly. "Like bloody dogs."

"Come inside, James, before you fall," cried a not-too-anxious female voice.

"Nearly finished, my sweet. Here I come!"

With a Tarzan-like cry, the figure fell backwards through the window. The men below remained still in the shadow of the wall for another five minutes, but no one else, clothed or naked, appeared to be interested in taking the air.

"Right," said Cess. "Jim, get on with it."

Jim advanced to his former spot on the grass.

"It's a bit chancy, old love," said Bertie diffidently.

"It's always chancy. But it'll bloody work," said Cess with a note of vicious challenge in his voice.

Bertie shrugged and didn't reply. But Joe had the feeling that he wished he was tucked up safe and warm in bed in whatever quarter of London he normally inhabited.

Now something else was happening above, this time on the second floor. From a window almost above that which had been the source of the recent hazardous micturition, something less noisome but just as puzzling descended. It was, Joe decided, a thin nylon line. To climb up, he supposed. Well, if they were expecting him to climb up that, they were going to be sadly disappointed.

Lord Jim had unwound from his shoulders the coils of rope he was carrying and now with swift efficiency tied one end of it to the end of the line dangling from the window. He waved his hand and it was rapidly hauled up. It was not, Joe now observed, a single length of rope, but two lengths, parallel. Joined at intervals of about eighteen inches by cross-lengths.

In short, or rather at length, a rope-ladder.

And Joe, with sinking heart, knew as an absolute certainty that they *were* going to expect him to climb that.

Above, a shadowy figure leaned out and signalled. This obviously meant the ladder was secure as Third Man now started forward at a nod from Cess and began to climb, the canvas bag now slung over his shoulders. He made it look quite easy, though Lord Jim helped a lot by grasping the bottom of the ladder and leaning back with all his strength to keep it as rigid as possible and away from the wall.

Bertie went up next, again with considerable agility. Then Cess with the other bag.

Joe looked at Lord Jim.

"After you," he said politely.

"Up," said Lord Jim, leaving Joe uncertain whether the word was directional or merely abusive. Either way, it seemed best to start the ascent.

He was between the first and second floors when his foot slipped off the rung, striking the wall behind and sending him swinging sideways in a desperate effort to regain his balance.

Below, Lord Jim, taken unawares by the move, was pulled off balance and staggered sideways in the wake of the ladder.

Above, his head protruding from the darkness of the wall like a gargoyle carved by a dyspeptic mason, Cess glared furiously down, the shine of his eyes and the twist of his mouth saying all he did not dare to put into words. Behind him, immeasurably distant, was the bright smear of the Milky Way.

The sight was inspirational and with a wrench that seemed to unzip his shoulder muscles, Joe heaved himself back into the perpendicular. Lord Jim took the strain again and he was able to hang there, untroubled for a moment, regaining his breath.

Untroubled, except in his mind where a strange vision he had just experienced swirled and misted like a hot spring.

Momentarily on his sideways swing, he had been able to look down through the lighted window on the first floor. His view had been obscured by steam, the source of which seemed to be a large sunken bath. Dimly through the mist he had glimpsed seven or eight apparently naked figures grotesquely crowded together in the water. Like a rugby team after a match.

A mixed rugby team.

One woman had been drying herself by the bath's edge. She had paused to take a drink from a handy bottle and as she did so, their gazes had locked. A look of mild surprise had flitted over her face, a hand had come out of the bath and seized her ankle, unbalancing her. And as she toppled with a Keaton-like lack of panic into the water, Joe had swung away.

Pondering these things, he resumed his ascent. Two pairs of arms reached down and dragged him violently up the last few feet, pulling him head first through the window and letting him fall uncushioned to the floor.

Dazed, he looked up. One of his helpers was, as he expected, Cess.

But the other was quite unexpected. A man he had never formally met but whose work he knew well and whose own picture had been prominent in the local press recently.

Your friendly local chemist and enthusiastic amateur photographer, Thomas Chubb.

CHAPTER IV

The room was in semi-darkness and filled with a strange chemical odour. Joe seized hold of a nearby table-leg to pull himself upright. It moved slightly under his weight and to his surprise Chubb prodded him none too gently with the gleaming toe of one of his patent leather bootees.

"Watch it! Christ, Cess, you didn't tell me you were going to be running a tour for the disabled as well. *Don't rock that bloody table!"*

"What's so precious?" mumbled Joe, standing up with the aid of an arm which he finally traced to Bertie.

"It's the man's pretty pictures, ducks," said Bertie.

"Dear God! Is he at that again?" marvelled Joe. "It's hardly any time since the trial."

The naked bodies in the bath began to fall a little more clearly into perspective. But much was still very puzzling. What was Chubb up to *developing* films here? Surely his role at Trevigore's party would be to *show* films? Dirty lot of sods they were, anyway. Christ, Lord Trevigore must be sixty-five if he was a day!

His thoughts were interrupted by Lord Jim's arrival. He hauled the rope-ladder up after him. Chubb switched on a red dark-room light which, if anything, made the room even more sinister, and busied himself among his equipment.

"Right, Tommy. What's the timetable?" said Cess very businesslike.

"Please keep your voice down, Cess!" said Chubb,

the busy little shopkeeper very much in evidence. This impression was heightened by the white apron he was wearing, doubtless as protection.

Or perhaps he's a mason, thought Joe. He looks the type.

But he noticed that Cess seemed ready to take instruction from Chubb and he wondered for a moment if the little pornographer could be the power he had sometimes sensed behind the throne.

"How long will you be?" asked Cess.

"Fifteen minutes. Less. Give me another fifteen after I leave, then you'll be OK."

"Guaranteed?" said Bertie with resigned disbelief.

"Oh yes," said Chubb. "I've been here before. Guaranteed. This is the best bit of the night. None of them's going to miss this."

"What's going on?" demanded Joe, happy that no violent movement seemed to be expected of him for at least half-an-hour.

Chubb smiled at him as though he'd just given short change. He was clearly a man happy in his work.

"Don't you know? It's a line of business I worked out myself. Very popular. It's just an extension of your usual blue-film party. I come along with all the gear. Right? The party's under way, everyone knows what it's all about, you follow me? I set up the camera, one or two lights, then when things really get going I start filming."

"You mean while they're . . .?" said Joe, fascinated.

"Right! It's a good set-up here. A big room with a gallery running round three sides. I'm right over the action. Lots of lateral movement and a zoom lens. I get the lot!"

"But that's the Rowley Room!" said Joe, now

deeply shocked. "The young pretender met the
fourth earl there and invited his help in 1745! A lot
of the woodwork in the gallery was carved by
Grinling Gibbons himself. And the balustrade at
the far end was originally an altar rail in an Aus-
trian monastery. You can't have an orgy *there*!"

"You'd be surprised where I've seen 'em at it!"
laughed Chubb. "Anyway. Eventually things cool
down a bit. It's a natural course of events. They
take a rest, have a shower, refreshments are served,
that kind of thing. While I shoot up here and develop the film. Then thirty or forty minutes later,
we reconvene, so to speak, and I run the film
through. Like I say, it's the best bit of the night.
Lots of laughs, watching themselves at it. And lots
of kicks too. It sets them all off again! You can
guarantee they'll all be on the job again, twice as
strong, before the film's finished running."

Chubb peered into one of his tubs, seemed satisfied and transferred the film it contained into the
next, swishing it about energetically.

"I thought it took hours to develop ciné film,"
said Joe.

"It does if you do a job. But anything goes for
this. Speed's the thing. I don't wash it properly or
owt like that, just a quick hypo-bath, then out it
comes."

He suited his actions to his words and soon had
a considerable length of film criss-crossing the room
from one corner to another.

"Rotten quality, but they don't mind. Now we'll
just dry it off."

He produced a portable hair-drier from under
the table and set it blowing, directing it up and
down the length of the damp film.

"I'm not trying for any Oscars," he went on.

"This'll be destroyed before I leave here, any road. They don't want it floating around, do they?"

"Tell me, Mr. Chubb," said Joe curiously. "Your trial. How'd you get off? You were guilty, weren't you?"

"As Judas bloody Iscariot" said Chubb with great satisfaction. "When you've got friends and neighbours . . ."

He tapped the side of his nose significantly.

"Get a move on, Tommy," said Cess in irritation. "You talk too much."

The fat little chemist relapsed into a sulky silence and Joe decided it was politic not to pursue his questioning any further.

Fifteen minutes later, Chubb was on his way.

"Remember," he said as he left. "Another quarter of an hour. See you around! But not around here, I hope!"

"Comedian," said Cess to the closed door.

The next fifteen minutes flew by. For Joe, at least.

"Time," said Cess, frighteningly quickly. "Now Joe, lad, here's your big moment. Take us to the Painted Gallery."

Twenty yards along the corridor, they passed a stairhead. From somewhere below came a burst of laughter. A wave of envy passed over Joe. Those bastards were enjoying themselves. A touch of the soft stuff. A drop of the hard stuff. Pheasant pâté, communal baths. Then a touch of the soft stuff again. And most of them would merely get an extra kick when they found the place had been robbed.

"Not lost, are we, Joe?" muttered Cess.

"Oh no. No," replied Joe, pushing open the door at the end of the passage. And, much to his relief, he wasn't any longer. This was familiar territory.

Two minutes later they stood at the door to the Painted Gallery.

Joe reached out to grasp the handle.

"Hold it," said Lord Jim.

"What for?" asked Joe. But he stood stock-still as he asked. Jim did not answer but backed slowly away from the door like a courtier leaving the presence of his king.

"Can you do it, Jim?" asked Cess impatiently.

"Wait a bit," replied Jim off-handedly.

Cess bit his lower lip, whether in annoyance at Jim's tone or mere impatience, it was hard to tell. But once again Joe noted with unease the slight crack in the man's hard surface.

Third Man had hung back at the end of the gallery in which they were standing. It was the gallery which Joe had wanted to get into when he was "casing" the house, and the memory made him realize why they had stopped here.

This was one of the points of contact between the private apartments and the open sector of the house. The door might well be locked. Old Trevigore would hardly want his drunken guests wandering around amongst his family treasures, though a man who could arrange an orgy in the Rowley Room was capable of anything. But it must be more than just a matter of locks, which would surely present no difficulty to this crooked lot.

"Visitors!" hissed Third Man, moving swiftly and silently to join them.

Bertie, who had been standing by a side-door, now pushed it open and the men surged in without hesitation, carrying Joe with them. He suddenly appreciated the casually expert way in which they had deployed themselves outside. Like cavalry escorting a wagon through Indian country. He alone, like the wagon, was too cumbersome and awkward for this kind of rapid instinctive action. He only hoped that, also like the wagon, he was an object to be protected.

Footsteps approached and passed. Lord Jim was on his knees, not a very great descent, peering through the crack in the door. Joe leaned forward to look too, digging his own knees hard into Lord Jim's back, but the little man didn't react.

It was Jock Laidlaw outside. Joe wondered at his presence. He could not see him very happily countenancing the kind of event at present going on in the Rowley Room.

Just now, however, he was behaving very oddly, standing on a chair (Georgian, solid, heavily ornamented, a good example of William Kent's influence) reaching up to the undistinguished gilded plasterwork which commenced some ten feet above floor level. Apparently satisfied he descended, returned the chair to its former position, carefully dusting it with his handkerchief, approached the door to the Painted Gallery, unlocked it and passed through.

It was a good five minutes before Cess gave the signal to move out. Immediately Lord Jim replaced the chair against the wall and climbed on to it. It was clear he could not reach anywhere near the point that Jock had been interested in. But he snapped his fingers, Third Man came and crouched alongside, and Jim stepped on to his back to get the extra height.

Joe winced at the sight.

"What's he after?" he asked.

"Interference switch," replied Bertie. "The full alarm-system's on the go here; you with me? But geezers like Haggis got to go through, so there must be a point where the alarm circuit can be broken without starting the whole bleeding orchestra. Naturally they don't put up a big notice advertising the fact!''

"But there are plenty of other doors leading to the public rooms. How did you know the switch'd be here?'' asked Joe.

Bertie looked mildly surprised.

"Why, that was you, Joe, old son! You told us, with all that stuff about wires and points and the control-room. He did well, didn't he, Cess?''

"Lucky for him,'' said Cess, unimpressed.

"Mind you, it's a stroke of luck your mate coming along. It'd have taken some finding, that thing, I reckon.''

They stared up at Lord Jim who was now performing a small operation on the plaster. Joe realized with a sinking heart that it would have mattered little if what had stood in his way had been an exquisite piece of woodcarving by Lobb or Davis.

"Why doesn't he just press the switch?'' he asked.

"Because when he does, a little red light will flash on and off in the control-room,'' said Bertie patiently. "Which is all right in the case of your mate, who's doubtless given them the word he's coming through. All kinds of nasty things would start happening if the guy at the console couldn't see any good reason why someone should be prowling around here. If Jim's right about this system, based on what *you* told him, of course, this little cottage would be shut up tight as a tin of baked beans in no time.''

"So what's he doing?'' asked Joe, feeling more and more unhappy.

"Making sure the little red light won't work. *Then* he'll press the switch.''

Thirty seconds later Jim leapt with surprising lightness to the floor.

"Done," he said.

Cess, who had been examining the lock closely, though without touching it, now started probing its depths as though he were being timed. Less than a minute passed before he stood up triumphantly and pushed open the door.

"Right," he said. "Got your shopping list, Bertie? Let's go."

"Hang on."

Bertie pulled the walkie-talkie from inside his jacket and switched it on.

"Blue blue blue," he said softly.

"Yellow yellow," came back the tiny distant voice.

"I'll leave it switched on to receive," said Bertie replacing it in his jacket.

"OK," said Cess, "but nothing's going to stop us now."

He took a deep breath and smiled brightly on them all, even Joe. His eyes were sparkling.

He's a manic-depressive, thought Joe. Oh God. I wish I were safe in bed a hundred miles away!

"Off you go, Joe. Show us how to get to the State Room."

The sooner things were done now, the sooner they would be out of the house and away, thought Joe.

He stepped through into the Painted Gallery, the others following. Third Man, still rubbing his back, closed the door gently behind him. As the rectangle of friendly light narrowed and disappeared, leaving them in what at first seemed like complete darkness, Joe realized for the first time just how valuable he was. With so many huge, uncurtained windows about the place, it was dangerous to use a torch, and the starlight that filtered through the glass was just sufficient to distort rather than reveal. It would be very easy to blunder around noisily, or even get completely lost. Unless you knew your way around blindfold. That had been his claim. Now it was going to be tested.

"Everyone ready," he whispered. "In line behind me please. Go when I tell you. *And do keep in line.*"

It's like taking 4S on an expedition, he thought gleefully. *Cess! Stop picking your nose. And take a hundred lines! And do stop playing with yourself, Jim. You'll stunt your growth!*

"Off we go," he said.

He had to admit that though he might know the way best, the others won all ends up when it came to moving silently. 4S had never been like this. Twice he paused and looked round, assailed by a frightening conviction that he was on his own. Each time the others were there, perfectly still, waiting to discover his reasons for pausing.

By using a couple of doors not on the sightseers' route he brought them to the suite of State Rooms in less than a couple of minutes. In fact, Cess grunted with surprise when Joe said, "Here we are!," and wasn't satisfied till he had prowled around and checked some of the furnishings against his list.

"Good work!" he said finally. "Jim. How're we fixed in here?"

Jim was crawling around the skirting with a pencil torch.

"It'll take a minute," he said. "If Joe's right."

"Me?" said Joe, frightened. "What's it got to do with me?"

"You got the info about the alarms, didn't you?" said Bertie reasonably.

"What if Joe isn't right? How long?"

"Five to ten years," said Lord Jim. "Depending on past record."

It was the nearest Joe had ever known Lord Jim come to a joke. Perhaps he was cracking under the strain as well.

"That should be OK," said Jim standing up, having performed a small operation on the wainscot.

"How do we know?" asked Bertie.

For answer, Jim climbed on to an early eighteenth-century walnut cabinet, exquisitely ornamented in gesso, and with difficulty lifted from the wall a large painting of a casual gent bearing a gun almost as long as he was and a brace of hares.

"It's OK," he said. "Do we want this?"

Bertie peered at the list.

"No," he said. "It's not here."

"What about you, Joe?" demanded Cess. "Any good?"

"I can't imagine anyone really wanting it enough to buy it illegally," began Joe.

"You mean no? Don't waste bloody time. Bertie, you shout out what's on your list, Joe, you show us where they are. Right?"

Lord Jim carefully replaced the picture on the wall and jumped down.

"Paintings first," said Bertie. "Van Dyck. The second earl. Van Dyck. Family group. The second earl, the countess, two children. Van Dyck. Madame Anne Shattoque. Jan van Huysum. Spring Flowers. Jan van Huysum. Roses and yew leaves. Adrian Brouwer. Peasants drinking. Jordaens. Diana bathing . . ."

"That's not here," said Joe. "I think the earl keeps it in his bedroom."

"We'll get it on the way back," said Cess. "Now let's work."

In for a penny, in for a pound, thought Joe and set about directing them to the chosen pictures with as much speed as possible. He felt unwell when he saw the first one rapidly removed from its frame, rolled up, and pushed into a cardboard cylinder produced from one of the canvas bags. But the feeling was soon overtaken by his growing sense of urgency and desire to be far away.

They took nine pictures in all, mostly what Joe would have expected. From pictures, they moved on to silver and porcelain, again being most selective. Obviously it was of first importance to satisfy the specific demands made by Bertie's customers. Each piece had a receptacle specially prepared for it in one of the bags. Someone had put in a great deal of preparatory work.

Joe's initial sense of the eeriness of the place had quickly worn off under pressure of the work. But gradually it returned. The dark figures moving silently through the darkened rooms assumed the air of predators; the family portraits on the walls seemed to take on new dimensions and loom fearfully, as though sculpted not painted; the whole atmosphere of the place seemed instinct with hostility.

They hate us! thought Joe. All those who had ever used these rooms, ghosts of haughty noblemen and forelock-tugging servants alike, they all hate us. Only the shuffling crowds of weekend sightseers might applaud, and they are too ghostlike in their reality to leave traces of their being here. But the others ... this place meant a way of life for them and we're wandering around it like a supermarket, picking up whatever we fancy and dropping it in the basket.

Only we don't intend to pay.

"The Round Chamber, Joe. Joe! Stop farting

about like a zombie. We're moving on to the Round Chamber. So move!"

Joe moved.

The Round Chamber figured large in Bertie's shopping list. It was a small domed room on the top floor, a dome echoed in the glass cupola which arched protectively over the central display-table. Around this table at a distance of about a yard ran a wooden barrier of a type much stronger than the usual single-stranded rope fence which elsewhere stopped profane feet from sullying ancient carpets. And there were always two stewards on duty here during the day. For in this room the hoi-polloi could cast their envious, amazed or, more often, exhausted gazes on some of the Trevigores' most precious knick-knacks.

It was an odd collection, whose only generic justification was that most of the items were unique examples of their kind.

More importantly to present purposes, they were all worth a lot of hard cash.

There was jewellery. An early medieval topaz brooch. Diamonds set in Italian gold. Rubies prised from their original settings—the fruits of empire.

There was some fine glass. A couple of pieces of Bohemian ruby by Kunkel, two dishes and a goblet in Bristol white, painted by Edkins. And other pieces whose historical associations more than compensated for their comparative commonness.

Cess was glancing at his watch now as Lord Jim started on his usual bloodhound performance outside the chamber, suspecting that this room might have some additional alarm safeguard built into the door.

"We're running late," said Cess through clenched teeth. "We've got to be out of here soon."

The time-limit, Joe decided, was set by the revelry going on back in the Rowley Room. Once that broke up, they were in all sorts of trouble. There would be people wandering around, cutting off their escape route back through the private apartments. Joe had no doubt that the stuff they had taken was leaving the Trevigore estate in Chubb's car. He hoped it was big enough for five passengers. No, six! For the first time in an hour he thought of Maggie sitting trussed up in the cave. Please God she was all right.

But the part of his mind (the larger part, he had to confess) concerned with personal survival had ferreted out one piece of comfort. Chubb's car. Of course! it wasn't a car; it was the van which had made its way so circumspectly along the park road, whose flashing lights, far from being an effort to scare away prowling lions, had been a signal to Cess. Plenty of room there.

Again he felt the comfort of being in the company of men whose professionalism was so apparent.

Jim declared himself satisfied and they entered the Round Chamber.

To Joe's surprise, Third Man, Cess and Bertie went straight to the glass cupola and lifted it off together. Expecting each second to hear the shriek of alarms, he backed slowly towards the door.

"Not to worry," said Lord Jim, noticing the movement. "It's safe enough. Try lifting one of those things off the cushion, that's when the trouble starts."

"Can't you fix it?" asked Joe, puzzled.

"No. It's not linked up to the main alarm-system at all. You put us on to it. Beneath that velvet there's a foam plastic cushion. Cells are impregnated with graphite which conducts an electric charge. Pressure on the cushion decreases the resistance. Lift something off, you increase the resistance. That triggers off the alarm."

This was Lord Jim at his most voluble.

"Does that mean we go home now?"

"No," said Jim, with a touch of pride. "We've got to lift things off without altering the pressure. Watch."

Bertie and Cess were crouched down over the table as though at some nerve-racking game. There were beads of sweat on both their foreheads.

Bertie held a small pair of padded tongs around the stem of a crystal goblet, while Cess stood poised at his shoulder with what looked like a lump of rough-cast plaster of Paris in his hand. On it was painted a large number 1.

"Weight equivalents!" said Joe. "That's why I had to find out those details."

"That's right, I hope you got them right. Cess drops his just as Bertie picks up his. They've been rehearsing for weeks."

Suddenly there was nearly disaster. Something slipped out of the front of Bertie's jacket, both men started back in shock, Lord Jim stepped swiftly forward and his outstretched hand caught the walkie-talkie about three inches above the velvet cushion.

"Christalmighty!" said Bertie.

"Oh my God!" said Cess.

Both men surprisingly seemed the better for their religious outbursts and returned immediately to their job, sparing no time on recrimination.

"Blue blue blue," murmured Lord Jim, testing the set.

"Yellow yellow," came the comforting reply. Jim switched off.

"Ahhh!" said Cess and Bertie simultaneously as

the lump of weighted plaster went down and the
goblet came up.

"Ahh," they said again in a different key as it
became apparent this was going to be the only
noise.

They did one more, just to show they could re-
capture the first fine careless rapture. Third Man
supplied the plaster substitutes from his canvas
bag and packed away the lifted objects with the
same meticulous care they all showed.

"Right, Jim," said Cess: "We'll finish off here.
Fifteen minutes at the most. You make your way
back to Tom's room with Joe. Here's his list. Pick
up what you can of it on your way. Remember,
Joe, you're on a percentage of this stuff. But don't
get greedy. We're running out of time. Fifteen minutes. Remember!"

"Right," said Jim, taking Joe's elbow and leading him through the door. The others were already
back at work before they left the Chamber.

"Nowt too easily broken," said Jim. "We've only
got these."

He held up a couple of large plastic carriers he
had taken out of one of the canvas bags. One of
them contained a roll of thin cotton wool for wrap-
ping purposes.

"I'll nick owt," Jim went on, "but I see no sense
in breaking."

A reasonable philosophy, thought Joe. A man
can do little more than set limits on the degree of
his criminality.

Despite their restricted carrying potential and
the need for haste, they had made substantial in-
roads into Joe's list by the time they re-entered the
private apartments. More and more Joe admired
the speed of movement and thought displayed by
the little square man. A new mood of buoyant

optimism had swept over him, symbolically rein-
forced by their emergence from the shadows into
the well-lit corridors and galleries of the private
sector.

"We'd best head back," said Jim, glancing at his
watch.

"No time for the private stuff?" said Joe almost
regretfully.

"No time," echoed Jim.

They retraced their steps carefully towards
Chubb's developing-room. There seemed to be no
sign yet of the party breaking up, though little
noise came floating up to the stairhead they had
listened at on their outward journey.

"They must be still at it," whispered Joe.

"Mebbe. Can you get us into that gallery Chubb
talked about?"

"I think so."

His navigational success that night had given
him new confidence and it was justified once more
when, a minute later, he pushed open a rather
squeaky door and peered in at a scene which Dante
might have regretted not inventing.

The Rowley Room was lit only by the shaft of
light from the ciné-projector which sent its images
down from the end of the gallery they were at on
to a large screen erected against the furthermost
wall. Chubb was standing by the projector peering
down with a melancholy mien at the activities
below. He turned, unsurprised, when Jim touched
his shoulder and stepped back into the shadows.

"All OK?"

"Yes. We thought we'd better get back. How
long's this going on for?"

"God knows!" said Chubb. "They must have been
getting injections! There's no sign of letting up

either. This is the third time I've run the bloody film."

Intrigued, Joe crawled forward to the gallery rails (the ex-monastic ones, he thought; the monks must be spinning!) and peered down.

The variety of activity below was at first fascinating. It was rather horrifying to realize that the general age-range seemed to be from fifty to seventy, but they were doing their best. Three or four couples were staging a kind of Grand National up and down the length of the room using furniture and the odd naked body as obstacles. An interesting type of Conga was being danced at the other side. Immediately below, two men were playing chess by candlelight, the board resting on the belly of a woman who appeared to be sleeping. It was at this point that Joe began to feel there was something a little self-conscious about the whole business. Real abandon seemed to have been abandoned and an upper-middle-class plastic substitute substituted. Over everything hung a stench of incense which seemed to be burning in your genuine incense-burners, probably looted by one of old Trevigore's noble forebears. Joe knew from his reading of the quality Sunday papers that this masked the smell of "pot" being smoked, and indeed several of those below were puffing gently away in a semi-stupor. No one anywhere seemed particularly close to orgasm. Joe almost wished the Hon. Jule and his generation were here to give the proceedings some life.

The film, however, was much better. Perhaps because it had been shot while everyone was in the first fine flush of sexual activity. Or perhaps it was just that its technical inadequacies all combined to produce an effect of stunning depravity. The definition and reproduction were, as Chubb had forecast, very poor. Added to this, there seemed to be an inordinate amount of dust in the projector which produced an impression of looking at the naked figures on the screen through an eye whose iris was being chewed away by carnivorous amoebae. Thirdly the height of the gallery meant that the image was being beamed downwards, striking the screen at an angle of about eighty degrees, producing a slight elongation of figure. Momentarily full-length shots appeared like El Greco martyrs, and the effect in male close-ups was often very flattering.

A hand gripped Joe's ankle and he felt himself dragged back forcibly from the edge of the gallery.

"Let's go," said Lord Jim. "The others will be here soon and we can get the stuff out to the van."

"Sooner the better," said Chubb. "This lot must be pretty well played out, surely!"

They left him as they had found him, like a tubby god staring down at his creation in great perplexity.

Once in Chubb's room, Joe felt able to relax. It was almost like coming home. Soon the others would be here, they would pack the loot away, pick up Maggie, then be off. Another thirty minutes, an hour at the most, would see him in his little VW, heading for bed. Could he include Maggie in that too? he wondered. She might be concerned about her parents missing her and worrying. She was that kind of girl. Nice.

Idly, he wandered over to the window and stared out to where the Blue Grotto lay in the darkness. He hoped to God she was all right.

His gaze dropped to the lawn below and instantly all his altruistic prayers for Maggie's well-being were forgotten.

"Jim!" he croaked. "Jim!"

The other joined him in a flash and stared down with him at the file of policemen moving inexorably across the lawn and into the house through a doorway below. His hand went into his pocket and pulled out the walkie-talkie.

"I switched it off," said Jim bitterly, flicking the control switch with his thumb.

"Red," it said distantly, tinnily. "Red red red red red . . ."

CHAPTER V

Through the centuries, from the author of the Book of Job via Francis Bacon and P. G. Wodehouse to Doctor Spock, keen observers of the human scene have noted the beneficent effects of a touch of adversity in bringing out the best in a man's character.

As far as Joe at this moment was concerned they could all get stuffed.

"What'll we do?" cried Joe, in shrill, sweaty terror.

"We've got to tell Cess."

Joe knew he should have felt shamed by the other's unselfishness. Perhaps he would later. But just at the moment he couldn't manage it. All it made him feel was endangered.

"There isn't time!"

Lord Jim didn't answer but rushed through the door. Joe followed, almost sobbing in panic. How the hell did they know? How? How? What had gone wrong?

In the corridor Lord Jim halted a moment and seized him by the shoulder. Joe wondered if he was going to advise him to play up and play the game, but instead he said, "You tell Chubb. Then get out if you can!"

Then off he went, pounding like a squat little bull along the corridor.

This time Joe did feel moved. Somewhere deep down beneath the welter of terror and panic something like an unselfish emotion stirred. Warn

Chubb. That was fair enough. A libation to the
gods of chance.

Then every man for himself, and to hell with
women and children!

Swiftly he made his way into the gallery of the
Rowley Room.

The film was still running. Amazingly, proceedings below seemed to have livened up again and a
lot of interesting developments had taken place in
the Conga chain. The smell of burning incense was
still as strong. Surely whoever called the police
must have warned this lot? But that was their
worry! Joe had problems of his own.

Chubb was sitting on a stool, his eyes closed,
disconsolately puffing a very smelly cheroot.

"For Christ's sake!" gasped Joe, "They're here!"

"Who? Cess? He'll have to wait," said Chubb
unimpressed.

"The police! It's the police!"

"Oh God!" Chubb was suddenly animated. He
leapt up and flung his cigar over the rails. There
was a shriek from below and an interesting varia-
tion of the Petroff defence was thwarted for ever as
the chessboard-bearer shook the butt-end from between her rather flabby breasts.

"The bastards! The bastards!" gabbled Chubb,
tearing the film forcibly out of the projector-gate.
"Where are they? How long have I got? I've got to
burn this!"

You try to do someone a favour, thought Joe
bitterly. And all he does is think of himself!

Thus musing, he retreated to seek his own salvation. But the full reward of an ironic God for trying
to help others was yet to be paid.

Lord Jim's huge hand caught him on the chest
and hurled him back into the gallery.

"What's wrong?" he cried.

"They're coming."

"Who?" demanded Joe, knowing full well who. "Cess?"

"The pigs. I nearly ran into them."

"Oh God. Why?"

"What's it matter? Your mate, that Scotch git's with them."

"Jock?" said Joe wonderingly, then with dawning comprehension, *"Jock!"*

Everything was clear. Jock's puritan conscience! His love of the house! Perhaps the police had contacted him after following Chubb. But whatever the full explanation, it spelt salvation.

"It's not us they're after," he said. "It's Chubb! And that gang of middle-aged delinquents down there! No wonder they're not bothered. They don't know—yet!"

Lord Jim's face did not reflect Joe's exultation.

"They'll be glad of us too," he said. "Let's get out of here. No, not that way!"

He dragged Joe back from the door and jammed a doubtful Chippendale chair against the handle.

"You know your way around," he said. "Get us out of here!"

There were three other doors leading from the gallery. The first two were locked. The third opened on to a small room or large cupboard with no other exit. In the middle of the floor knelt Chubb, cigarette-lighter in hand, desperately blowing at a slowly uncoiling heap of film. He looked up in despair as they opened the door.

"Bloody non-inflammable film" he said. "Are they here?"

"Nearly," said Jim glancing back at the door, whose handle was being shaken vigorously. "Come on, expert! Where now?"

Joe's mind raced madly. Flight was impossible.

Concealment then? Where? Not in here with the incendiary Chubb!

"Paper? Got any paper?" demanded the chemist hopelessly as his attempted bonfire went out again.

"No. *Here*! Use this!"

In a fever of excitement Joe dragged his black sweater over his head and began to undo his trousers at the same time. Jim started back as though threatened by a madman.

"Merge with the background!" yelled Joe. *"Come on!"*

It said much for the speed of Jim's mind and more for the speed of his reactions that he was naked first.

Leaving Chubb thrusting matches into their nylon masks, they straddled the balustrade of the gallery, hung free for a moment, and, as the Chippendale chair gave way, spilling a gaggle of constables into the gallery, they dropped on to the Conga chain below.

The confusion was less than might have been imagined. The arrival of the police (now visible also at the downstairs doors) had not yet impinged upon the revellers, who seemed disposed to regard the descent of two new men as a kind of manna from heaven. Lord Jim especially, squat, muscular, and generously endowed, was an object of great admiration. Joe broke away from the pack, staring desperately around for an uncovered exit. There was none to be found. The police still hesitated where they stood, probably struck with the same wondering fascination he had felt on first being confronted by the scene. At least there was no sign of Jock. He'd probably keep very much in the background. Whatever his part in summoning the law, he would see no reason to advertise it.

A hand placed itself very familiarly upon his

body. Startled he spun round. Standing beside him, still naked, was the woman whose gaze he had met as he swung on the ladder outside the bathroom window. She was about forty, (young for this company) well-made, a bit dishevelled but not unattractive.

"Haven't we met?" she said with a smile.

"Perhaps we bumped into each other in the crowd," he answered brightly.

They'd have to bluff it out. If they could. The police would want names, addresses. Was it an offence to have a private orgy? God alone knew. But the "pot" . . . They'd be on to that in a flash.

"I don't think so. I usually remember," she said, smiling boldly. He nodded politely and turned away but she maintained her gentle grip on him. It was not unpleasant. But there was no time for pleasure.

"*Ladies and gentlemen!*"

Someone was shouting. A few heads turned.

"*Ladies and gentlemen!*"

It was one of the police in the gallery. The voice was oddly familiar. The revellers were slowly becoming aware of the presence of the constabulary. One or two well-bred shrieks went up.

"*Ladies! Gentlemen!*"

Joe looked up this time. Dressed in plain clothes, his hands cupped round his mouth, a white-haired man was doing the shouting.

"Police!" cried the woman, releasing him.

Prince! thought Joe. Sergeant bloody Prince! There'd be no bluffing him.

He flung his arms round the woman, who was retreating, probably in search of clothes, and pulled her down on top of him behind a chaise longue.

"My God!" she said struggling. "I'll try most things. But not in front of policemen!"

"Why not?" said Joe, trying to infuse passion into his voice. "It's not illegal."

"Ladies and gentlemen. I am a police officer. Please stay where you are. We would like you all to help us in our inquiries." Prince let an audibly ironic note drift into his voice.

"Get—off—me!" choked the woman out of the side of her mouth as Joe went through the motions of kissing her, though without any real conviction. Suddenly she applied her former grip. For one rather frightening moment he thought she was capitulating. Then she twisted, hard.

His long surprisingly high-pitched shriek triggered off a general uproar. Four or five women made a rush for the doors and grappled with the uniformed policemen, who gave every evidence of enjoying their duties. Prince shouted instructions from above. And another voice, not so strong, but more imperious, more attention-grasping, also began to demand quiet.

Joe looked up from the bent-double position which seemed to give him most ease. Standing on a fine mahogany table, white hair flowing back from a noble brow, eyes flashing, arms upraised, a most prophet-like mien, was Lord Trevigore, tenth earl of that ilk.

Like nearly all his guests, he was stark naked.

"My friends!" he said. "Dignity! I beg of you! Compose yourselves. You are in my house and no harm shall befall anyone who has come under my protection."

He now raised his face towards Prince. He was very well preserved for a man of his age.

"You, whoever you are. I've no doubt that you believe you have some legal justification for this intrusion. Well, we'll put this to the test. But it's not fitting to discuss the matter here in front of my guests. Damn it, man, have you no sense of responsibility? Of common decency? There are ladies present!"

It was a fine attempt in the circumstances. But Prince was unimpressed.

"We don't mind the ladies, my lord. If they have clothes with them, they may get dressed. But nobody leaves this room without first proving their identity to my officers."

"How do those without clothes prove their identity, may I ask?" said Trevigore with heavy irony. He had a beautiful line in aristocratic scorn, thought Joe, admiring despite himself.

Prince's answer to this interesting question was unexpected. He opened his mouth and let out the most hideous, cacophonous, ear-rending scream Joe had ever heard. At least, so it seemed for the long seconds it took for his mind to come to some tenuous compromise with this massive offensive of noise.

He felt himself seized by the shoulder and cowered away, fearing another attack from the woman. But it was Lord Jim, brushing off a gaggle of excited and frightened women.

"It's the alarm!" Jim mouthed.

Cess and the others! thought Joe. After so much care, someone must have blundered.

The police at the doors were obviously uncertain what to do. There was no chance of any instructions shouted from the gallery penetrating the din. But they were still maintaining a very effective barrier.

Things seemed worse than ever. What little chance of a bluff there might have been would disappear once the robbery was discovered. It would need a miracle to get them out of this, thought Joe bitterly. And miracles had been scarce this year.

He turned his face accusingly to heaven. And felt the first spots of rain.

Others felt them too. It was no illusion. The first cold drops were accelerating into a steady downpour. It was like being thrust unexpectedly under a cold shower and a general outcry arose as the chilly water jetted against the naked bodies all around.

The explanation came as suddenly. Above on the gallery a door burst open and a small fat figure staggered out to rest up against the railings in a great puff of black smoke. But he did not look unhappy.

Chubb had succeeded in destroying his film. But the fire he had started had triggered off the ultra-sensitive reactions of the new sprinkler system.

"Fire!" someone cried.

"Fire; Fire!" Joe and Jim echoed with a common enthusiasm. *"Fire!"*

There was no stemming the rush for the door this time. The policemen's hearts were no longer in it and Joe let himself be carried out into the corridor on the height of the naked tide. Jim was close behind, like all experts ready to defer to the expertise of others in different fields. The field in this case being the geography of Averingerett. Under his arm which was muscled like that of Popeye the Sailorman, he carried a bundle.

"What's that?" yelled Joe above the hubbub of the fleeing matrons.

"Clothes," said Jim. "We can't get home like this."

That a normal humdrum existence still waited for him outside this madhouse, that it was yet possible he might return freely to it, these were thoughts Joe himself had long since banished from his mind. Now Lord Jim's words seemed like a reaffirmation of basic tenets of human morality. He could have kissed him heartily, which was more or less what a purple-rinsed grandame with a nice line in half-nelsons was trying to do. One good turn deserves another, and he dislodged her from Jim's back with a heavy chop to the kidneys, then steered his friend (for so he now thought of him) out of the mainstream of the carnal torrent through a familiar door.

It led to the Book Room, which Joe resented more than any other part of the house. The sprinkler system was operating with less enthusiasm here, mere summer-shower force, though still icy cold.

"Where now?" grunted Jim.

"Through that door. Across the gallery. Looks out over the gardens," Joe panted in reply.

"Right," said Jim pushing open the door. Joe hesitated, looking round the crowded shelves with love and envy. He was glad to see the water jets were hardly touching the majority of books. The smell of old leather and paper brittle with age hung like sweet perfume on every side, stronger in the damp. He knew he should go, but for a second all this was his and he was loath to give it up for ever.

"Bugger it!" he said finally and with a precise remembrance which took its images from the heart not the mind, he plucked down from a high shelf the copy of *Political Justice* he had coveted so long.

Like Eve and the apple in the garden, he thought ironically.

The serpent, in duplicate, was waiting in the gallery.

Standing between Lord Jim and the windows were two very solid policemen looking fairly unimpressed by the aggressive stance of the squat nude in front of them. Water dripped comically from the peaks of their helmets.

"Evening all," shrilled Joe, forcing a fatuous grin on to his face. "Ah, there you are, Jim old son. What's new on the Rialto?"

Second-rate pastiche Bertie Wooster, he thought gloomily. But it would have to do.

"May we have your name, sir?" asked one of the policemen politely.

"Of course. Like my telephone number as well, perhaps. Eh? Eh?" Joe laughed inanely. "Trevigore's the name. Julian of that ilk."

The policemen exchanged enigmatic glances.

"Oh," said the policeman. "One of the family, are you, sir?"

"That's damn sharp of you, Officer," said Joe. "Damn sharp. Well, we'd best be tootling along, I dare say. Come on, Jim."

He turned and moved back into the Book Room, Jim close behind. For a second he thought it might work. Then a fastidious finger tapped his bare shoulder.

"Excuse me, sir," said the talking policeman. "I must ask you to go with us and prove your identity to the officer in charge."

"But I've told you who I am!" said Joe with as much outrage as he could manage, thinking gloomily what unlikely-looking ornaments of the peerage he and Lord Jim were.

Talking-Policeman was adamant and Silent-Policeman looked ready to wade in with those actions which according to tradition speak louder than words.

"Oh, all right," said Joe.

He looked in silent appeal at Jim. All his bluff was going to do was carry them back to trouble. Any other answer to this situation had to come from the professional.

The professional rose to the occasion by the simple expedient of sinking his fist in Talking-Policeman's belly and his knee in Silent-Policeman's groin. Their roles were instantly reversed, TP opening and closing his mouth goldfish-like, producing no sound; SP sinking to his knees muttering, "Holymarymotherofgodohyoubastard." Joe would not have believed that such menace could be reduced so swiftly to such impotence. But it was clear that, like the phoenix, they would shortly rise more terrible than before and he didn't want to be around.

The alarm sirens stopped as they reached the window in the gallery, though not the sprinklers. For a moment the sudden silence seemed a beautiful gift from whatever god might be overlooking their activities. Then it was broken by the desperate shrilling of a police-whistle behind. Silent-Policeman was finding a better use for his breath than mere prayer.

Happily the window only caused a little delay, though this was enough to permit Talking-Policeman to come in with his whistle, which was a semi-tone lower, providing a not displeasing counterpoint to the other. As they fell out into the garden, doors were slamming distantly within as the police in the house tried to reach the source of the SOS whistling.

But worse, round the corner of the house, though some considerable distance away, appeared a couple of tall-helmeted figures.

"Come on," said Jim, breaking into a trot, his short legs covering a surprising amount of ground.

Joe needed no encouragement. Whistles were sounding outside now and there were cries of instruction and direction floating up into the night air behind them. The ground was hard and, now they had cleared the lawn, stony beneath his bare feet. And the shrubbery they forced their way through seemed to consist entirely of stinging nettle and briar rose. His imagination shrank from imagining what it was doing to his body.

The initiative was back with Joe now as the topographical expert and Jim followed the twists and turns of his chosen route without comment.

We make a good team, thought Joe with surprise. Joe and Jim. Burglaries by appointment. Book early to avoid disappointment.

He almost smiled at the thought and instantly this brief flash of merriment seemed to be externalized. Which was absurd, of course.

"Christ!" said Jim, who had suddenly become clearly visible.

"Christ indeed," said Joe.

Some smart copper had switched on the floodlights used to illuminate the house and gardens on certain special occasions. *Son et lumière.* And the extra *lumière* was matched by a perceptible increase in *son.* Pausing in the concealing shadows of the azalea grove, they looked back at the brightly-lit scene.

There were displeasingly large numbers of policemen in sight, but the bulk of the extra noise came from Lord Trevigore's party guests who, driven by the image of fire and the reality of water, had spilled out of the house on to the lawn. Some were struggling desperately into odd garments which they had rescued, and disputes over ownership seemed to be breaking out.

Joe was reminded of the bundle still tucked under Jim's arm. It seemed a good moment to see what they had got.

"Let's dress," he said to Jim, who nodded agreement as though he'd been invited to change for dinner.

Division of the spoils was easy. It had not seemed the kind of party to which anyone would wear tails, but somebody had. A small thin man by their fit, thought Joe as he struggled into the trousers. Jim's bulk made them quite impossible for him. Fortunately the small thin man in tails must have been taken by the charms of a corpulent woman in a purple-flowered trouser-suit.

Joe laughed so much he had to sit down. There was a hysterical note in his laughter, he realized, but also a great deal of real amusement. He laughed so loud that it was some time before he realized that someone else was sharing the joke. And it wasn't Jim.

A figure stood among the azaleas, darkly outlined, shaking with amusement.

"What's going on?" it finally spluttered. "You two . . . oh dear! . . . Old Mother Riley meets the Western Brothers!"

"Maggie!" said Joe. "What are you doing . . . how did you get out . . .?"

For a second the fear flashed across his mind that he had been wrong about Jock, that it was Maggie who'd brought the police. He crossed to her protectively, fearing Jim might be ready to exact vengeance.

But Maggie was smiling almost fondly at the other.

"He untied me," she said. "Made me promise to stay in the cave. I'm sorry, though. There was so much noise, and lights, I just had to come out to see what was going on. What *is* going on?"

"Later," said Joe. "At the moment what we've got to do is move out of here."

"And quick," said Jim, pointing down the garden. A line of policemen was moving steadily towards the azalea grove. With them was Jock Laidlaw.

"They've seen us," said Joe. "And Jock'll have told them that we can only get as far as the barrier round the park."

"There must be another way out," cried Maggie, clinging to him. It was comforting that she identified herself so completely with the hunted, not the hunters, but not the kind of comfort that was of any practical use.

"Only the main gate out of the car-park and no one's going to get through that," said Joe.

"The cave," said Jim, hitching up the flared bottoms of his silk trousers and setting off through the grove.

"What's he mean?" asked Maggie as they followed him.

Joe merely grunted and shook his head. His own interpretation of Jim's words was not one he cared to share.

It was confirmed, however, the moment they entered the cave and their eyes grew accustomed to the dimmer light. Jim was down on his knees, scrabbling away at the loose rock Bertie had so carefully packed into the gap above the single great boulder blocking the passage. The loose stuff came out easily and Jim was able to reach both arms into the dark hole and take a grip on the boulder. Then, shifting his position so that he was no longer kneeling, but squatting with his feet braced against the sides of the cave, he began to heave.

For a moment nothing happened. Every line of his body showed tremendous strain, all the greater because of the perfect stillness of the scene. In his purple trouser-suit, thought Joe, he looked like a piece of butch statuary, symbolizing something quite unimaginable.

Then the balance was broken. There was a tearing, grating noise and the boulder began to move.

Joe exhaled noisily, realizing for the first time he had been holding his breath.

Behind him, Maggie spoke quietly, thoughtfully.

"Am I right in guessing this cave leads through into the park?"

"Yes," said Joe.

"Which is full of lions?"

"Not full," said Joe firmly. "A dozen. Twenty. And it's a very big park."

"Very big. And we've got to cross it in the company of a dozen, or twenty lions, and get out of the other side."

"Yes," said Joe.

Jim had got a great deal of way on the almost spherical boulder now and was retreating before it in a series of little kangaroo jumps. His purple silk had split embarrassingly across the seat.

"Oh no!" said Maggie. "It's crazy! We can't! Don't be so bloody stupid!"

The boulder came to a halt in the widest part of the cave. The eye of the black tunnel which Jim had unplugged leered uninvitingly at them. Jim rose to his feet, rubbing his back.

"He'll get five years," he said unemotionally. "I'll get fifteen."

He said no more but crouched down and began to move into the depths of the cave.

"He's right," said Joe hopelessly. "I've got to try it. But you'll be all right, Maggie. You stay. They can't touch you."

He kissed her passionately.

"This afternoon," he said. "In the field. That wasn't usual. I was worried about all this."

"So?" she said drawing back. "Why are you telling me?"

At first he didn't know. Then suddenly he did.

"If I get away, if things ever get back to normal," he said in a rush, "will you marry me?"

For answer she pushed him forward into the tunnel.

"Move," she said. "Let's catch up with Jim."

He twisted his head to look at her.

"But you're not coming . . .?"

"You may be my fiancé," she said, "but that doesn't mean I trust you. I've seen you in action and I'm not letting you out of my sight. So move!"

Joe's heart was singing with joy as they went forward towards the patch of lightness which marked the other end of the cave. He felt light-headed and had to take deep breaths of the stuffy, musky air to satisfy the oxygen needs of his racing blood. The smell of the air reminded him of something. Whatever it was, it would be associated for ever in his mind with this glorious moment.

An arm like a shillelagh came out of the shadows and impeded his further progress.

"Hold it," whispered Lord Jim. "And keep quiet."

He led them a few steps farther forward and pointed. In the shadows ahead something stirred momentarily. A cavernous mouth opened, yawned. A whole group of shadows rearranged itself. Then became still.

Between the three fugitives and the mouth of the cave there lay sleeping four extremely large lions.

CHAPTER VI

It was Maggie who rose to the occasion, Joe observed with pride. Her cold doubts about the escape route seemed to have disappeared completely in the glow of their new relationship.

"Cats," she said. "They're just cats. Like Vardon."

Absurdly the mention of Vardon brought tears to Joe's eyes. He would be worried. He hated Joe to be out late, though he refused to organize his own outgoings and incomings to any fixed schedule.

"Come on," said Maggie.

So saying she stepped lightly forward and walked past the sleeping beasts without a glance in their direction. At the mouth of the cave she stopped and beckoned impatiently.

With an inward prayer, spoken with that fervour known only to agnostics in trouble, Joe moved forward. He was almost past them when his foot sent a stone rattling along the cave floor.

The biggest of the beasts, obviously the daddy of this happy family, raised his noble head slightly from the cushion of his paws (each, to Joe's jaundiced gaze, equal in terms of bedding to a sizeable bolster) and opened his left eye.

Joe froze, uncertain whether to try to stare the beast out (as recommended by the *Boys' Own Paper*) or to affect complete indifference by looking elsewhere. Dogs, he knew, could be made to feel very uncomfortable and aggressive if you stared hard at them. Vardon, on the other hand, often locked eyes with him for minutes on end, sometimes to remind him it was time for food or bed, but more often with the dispassionate gaze of a philosopher, trying to reach some comprehension of the strange object before him.

He prayed that it was philosophy not food that was going through this lion's head. Whatever it was took a long time, but finally, as though deciding that Joe was an illusion created by some gobbet of undigested beefsteak, the animal shook his head slightly and went back to sleep.

Joe was shaking when he reached the comfort of Maggie's arms. Behind him Jim came through at a fast trot.

It was, they theorized later, the rustle of the purple silk which did it. Like a snake on the cave floor. Even lions wouldn't like snakes.

Whatever it was, with one accord as though at a pre-arranged signal, all four lions (mummy, daddy and two nearly full-grown sons, or daughters— there was no time to check) leapt up and started roaring mightily.

Joe's first impulse was to run.

"Hold it," yelled Jim joining them with a mighty bound. "They'll come after us."

Where Jim derived his dubious knowledge of lion-lore, Joe did not know. Perhaps he had always wanted to be a lion tamer. Now, before they could stop him, he bent down, picked up a sizeable lump of rock and hurled it at the nearest lion, catching it painfully on the chest. It stepped back, snarling out promises of savage retribution. Joe and Maggie joined the onslaught now, flinging rocks, pebbles, bones (there were a distressing number of these around) sticks and abuse at the now thoroughly roused beasts. It seemed certain to Joe that the light must dawn eventually, the animals would realize what laughably puny opposition they were up against and the counter-attack would bowl them over in seconds.

In fact, the end came as suddenly as he had feared. But it was quite unexpected.

Daddy, who had looked like potentially the biggest threat of all, simply decided that enough was enough, turned tail and disappeared into the depths of the cave. The other three glanced after him, glanced at each other in disillusion, then, with flicks of the tail which clearly said *"What the hell!"* they went after him. In a couple of seconds they had disappeared completely from view.

"We've won!" said Joe joyfully.

"Oh God," said Maggie in horror. "They've gone through!"

Lord Jim went scrambling up the rocky mound of the grotto, closely followed by the other two. It took some time to find a vantage point from which they could see through the thorn hedge and the double-wire fence which even up here acted as the park boundary, but when they did it provided a sight worth seeing.

The brightly-lit gardens were buzzing with activity. The naked and semi-naked guests had been shepherded into a fairly orderly group in the centre of the lawn and clearly some kind of identification parade had been taking place.

Equally clearly the search party had made contact with the lions, for suddenly, down from the upper reaches of the garden, shouting high-pitched warnings, losing their helmets in their flight and leaving them where they lay, came a dozen or more constables. The group on the lawn seemed to freeze. One figure stepped out from among them (it looked like Prince) and seemed to be shouting angrily at the running policemen, who began to slow down. A couple even turned as if to go back for their helmets.

Then the four lions broke out of the shadows of the azalea grove.

The light seemed to take them by surprise and their forward impetus carried them almost to the edge of the lawn before they halted. For a moment they stood still, the police stood still, the naked and half-naked guests stood still.

Then, as though at a signal, they let out one magnificent, arrogant, concerted roar and loped away to the side, passing (as though deliberately) before one of the floodlights sited behind the lawn, so that their shadows were cast mightily on the façade of the house.

After that everybody was running. And from this distance it sounded as if everybody was shrieking. For between five and ten seconds the gardens looked as if they were filled with two or three hundred panic-stricken men and women. Then, suddenly, like a piece of trick photography, they were gone. The lions too. Everything still. Not a sign of movement.

Except . . .

"Look," said Jim, pointing. "On the roof. To the far right. See?"

Joe saw. Some figures, two? three? detached themselves from a huge chimney-stack at the stables end of the house and disappeared behind the parapet which overlooked the car park.

"Cess? Bertie?" he said.

"Who else. Listen!"

Another noise now began to rise against the night's stillness. A siren, distant as yet but coming fast.

"Police?" asked Maggie.

"No," said Jim. "Fire. There'd be a direct alarm-link with the fire station."

"You know," said Joe thoughtfully, "what with the fire-engine coming through—and they'll probably call in the rangers off the gates to deal with the lions in the garden—I reckon we might be able to get out of here without having to hack our way through this kind of stuff."

He indicated the wire and the thorn with distaste.

"You could be right," said Jim.

"Come on," said Maggie.

He was right. The god of thieves must have decided they had had enough of accidents and disasters for one day. Suddenly everything was plain sailing. They reached the main gate at the bridge without sight or sound of another lion. As anticipated, there was a tremendous amount of activity at the gate, which was being left wide open for minutes on end. To slip through was absurdly easy and the gate at the other end of the bridge no longer seemed to be manned at all.

They walked for an hour, agony in bare feet, before they felt it was safe for Maggie to try the main road. Dressed as they were, it was clearly dangerous for either of the men to be seen, but Maggie was able to repair most of the ravages caused by the night and appear quite presentable. Joe gave her careful directions to where he had left his car, and where the key was hidden. Fifteen minutes later, crouched in a ditch they watched her climb into the cab of a lorry, and thirty minutes after that she was back with the VW.

"We'll have to watch for police-checks," warned Jim.

"Hang on," said Joe, reaching into the glove-compartment. "Here we are. There won't be any checks the way we go."

He produced Cyril Solstice's route-map.

The wisdom of God was unquestionable, thought Joe. Nothing was created without purpose. Even Cyril's strange obsession turned out to be merely another small piece in the great jigsaw of fate.

Not even the necessity of sending his lovely little car splashing through two fords could interfere with this new optimism.

But the rest of the night was not yet ready to pass entirely without incident.

They garaged the car and made their way swiftly through the back door of Joe's house. This necessitated passing Alice's door and to Joe's horror it opened as they passed and Alice appeared in her dressing-gown. She looked enigmatically at Maggie, at Joe in his borrowed tails, at Jim in his silk trouser-suit.

"Go on up," said Jim.

Joe and Maggie obeyed, Joe looking back uneasily from the landing, fearful lest Lord Jim should be offering some threat of violence to his neighbour. They looked to be in close confabulation, then Jim suddenly turned on his naked heel and to Joe's consternation marched out of the front door. Quickly he ushered Maggie into the flat and peered out of the window.

Parked almost opposite the house was the blue Cortina. Jim approached it, wrenched open the door and leaned inside. There was evidence of violent movement. After a minute or slightly longer, Jim withdrew, slamming the door with a ferocity which must have done some damage, the car engine started up and, somewhat erratically, the vehicle moved away into the darkness.

"What was all that about?" asked Maggie.

"God knows," said Joe. "And He won't tell."

Jim was as unforthcoming as God when he reappeared, accepting with a grunt the ill-fitting clothes Joe put at his disposal and refusing an invitation to spend what remained of the night in the flat.

"I'll take these," he said bundling up their borrowed robes. "Sooner they're got rid of, the better."

"What about Cess and the others?" asked Joe with not altogether spurious anxiety. "Shouldn't we try to find out . . .?"

"Why? If they got out, we'll learn. If they didn't, we'll hear too. Lay low."

With a polite nod to Maggie, Jim passed silently through the door.

"I hope he's all right," said Maggie.

"He will be. What about you?"

"What about me?"

"Well, er, are you *staying*, or do you have to go?"

"I'm beginning to wonder about you," said Maggie looking at him coldly. "Ever since I started teaching, you've given the impression that you'd like to be ripping the black lace off me all the time. Recent events make me wonder if it isn't just an act. Anyway *I'm* going to bed. What you do's your own business."

She disappeared into the bedroom, reappearing a moment later barely covered in the black lace.

"Of course," she said. "It is your flat. And you're entitled to ask me to leave."

At nine-thirty the next morning there was a prolonged ringing of the doorbell. The events of the previous twenty-four hours, (not least, the events of the previous four or five,) had enveloped Joe in a cocoon of fatigue which it took considerable willpower to shake off.

But it fell away like a transvestite's bosom when he saw who it was at the door.

"Come in, Sergeant Prince," he said, shakily.

"I'm sorry to trouble you so early," said Prince with a smile. "Thought you might be playing golf this morning and I'd catch you before you went."

"No," said Joe. "I was asleep."

"Oh? Late night?"

"Relatively," said Joe cautiously. "What can I do for you?"

"Have a nice time at Averingerett yesterday?"

"Very. Thank you. Why do you ask?"

Prince ran his fingers through his white hair.

"You see, I got out to Averingerett after all. Funny how things work out, isn't it? That call I got to go into the station. It was because of a tip-off."

"Tip-off?" said Joe, trying to assess the amount of interest he should realistically be showing.

"Yes. Can't give you details. But it was about a man we've been after for some time. In connection with pornographic films."

"Oh, Chubb," said Joe with relief. It had been Jock after all.

"Why do you say that?" demanded Prince. Belatedly Joe realized his error.

"Why, well, Chubb . . . It was in the paper. Our senior mistress, you know her, Onions, was on the jury. So we heard all about it."

"I see," said Prince. "Oddly, when we got there, we found there was a robbery in progress."

"Robbery?"

"That's right."

"That's remarkable," said Joe. "Catch anyone?"

Prince eyed him with what might or might not have been irony.

"Not yet," he answered. "But we live in hope. You see anything odd while you were there?"

"Me? No. Why do you ask?"

"Well, you're a bit of an expert aren't you? We reckon these boys must have stopped behind after afternoon closing. And they seemed to know what they were after, judging from what we found in their bags."

"Bags?"

Prince nodded.

"Bags. They were in a hurry to get away, it seems. My men saw a couple of them, so there's a chance of identification."

This was like a jolt to the solar plexus.

"Though they were naked. And wet."

"Your men?" he managed.

"Makes a difference," said Prince ignoring him. "Hard to hold a satisfactory identification parade. Hurt your legs, have you? That looks sore."

Joe glanced down at his bare legs protruding from his Japanese bath-robe. He couldn't have been altogether wrong about the prevalence of briar-rose last night. There were several nasty scratches plainly evident. Involuntarily he pulled the robe more tightly round him to hide his body.

"It's nothing," he said. "My cat. Had a scare. Can be quite vicious when he's got the wind up."

On cue, Vardon appeared from the kitchen. He had been most offhand a few hours earlier, his normal reaction at being left by himself longer than he felt was suitable. But now he oozed conde-scending forgiveness and jumped on Joe's lap, purring loudly.

"He looks very vicious," said Prince. "Maggie enjoy the trip?"

"Oh yes. Very much," said Joe, glad to be back on what seemed like firm ground.

"That's odd," said Prince. He didn't carry on, but started wandering round the flat looking carefully at the few paintings and ornaments Joe possessed.

He wants me to ask why, thought Joe suddenly uneasy. What's wrong? What have I said that's wrong?

The ground began to lose some of its firmness.

"Why?" he asked hopelessly.

"Well, your friend Laidlaw. You saw him yesterday afternoon, didn't you? It came up last night, quite by chance. He didn't recollect anyone being with you. In fact, he was certain you were by yourself."

Jock. Oh, the bastard! But why blame Jock? It was his own fault. He remembered telling Jock just that.

Prince turned from a close study of a Picasso print. Either he didn't like Picasso or he had decided that the friendly front had had its day. Both perhaps.

"So, was he wrong?" he said. "Or were you wrong, Joe? Perhaps Maggie wasn't with you. Perhaps you just didn't like to tell me you'd had a quarrel?"

This almost contemptuous offer of an excuse was the worst thing that had happened yet. It meant Prince was very nearly confident enough to come right out in the open. Once he did that, Joe suspected he would not retreat till he had dug up every last scrap of truth.

"Joe!" shouted Maggie from the bedroom. "Bring us a cup of coffee, there's a love."

Prince froze where he stood, a look of complete surprise on his face.

He didn't expect this, thought Joe. This could knock most of his little theories about me to hell and back. If only Maggie doesn't put her foot in it! I've got to have a quick word with her somehow.

He smiled apologetically to Prince and turned to the bedroom door, but it was too late. It was open and Maggie stood yawning widely, his silk dressing-gown draped loosely around her. It was a magnificent sight. Then she saw Prince.

"Maurice!" she said, pulling the dressing-gown tightly round her, producing an effect almost as voluptuous.

"Hello, Maggie," he said dully.

Poor sod, thought Joe. It's been a real shock for him. Professionally *and* personally perhaps.

Maggie turned the full summer-dawn smile on at Joe.

"Darling, shall we tell him? Hell, he must have guessed! Maurice, Joe and I are going to be married! Isn't it great! You'll have to come to the wedding, won't he, Joe?"

"Sure," said Joe. "He can give us a pair of handcuffs."

"It all happened at Averingerett yesterday. It's a fantastic place, you'll have to go there some time, Maurice."

Don't push it! thought Joe.

"Though it was absolutely packed. We lost each other for a while in the crowd. At least, I was lost. It turned out Joe had been supping beer in the head steward's room while I was wandering around looking for him!"

"Well, congratulations," said Prince. "Maggie. Joe. I hope you'll be happy."

He smiled uncertainly. Watch him! Joe told himself.

"I expect you were out celebrating last night," he said at the door.

Joe's mind raced to try to spot the drift of the question. But Maggie was well ahead of him.

"Oh no," she said. "It was too crowded at Averingerett so we drove off, found a quiet lay-by to park the car and took our picnic-hamper with us into a wood. We must have been there hours. Absolutely hours. Time just flew."

She fluttered her eyelashes coyly.

Beautiful, thought Joe. He should have spotted it! Once before the VW's number had been taken and its position casually noted by some passing cop. Outside the Bell. It was odds-on that the same thing had happened at some point the previous evening. And Prince had noticed it. And decided to check.

Vardon, who had been looking alertly at each of the speakers in turn, evidently decided that it would be fun to get in on this fool-Prince act.

He yawned, licked his left paw, jumped down from Joe's lap, turned and sank his claws into Joe's shin as though into a scratching post.

"I'd watch that cat," said Prince after Joe's scream had died down. "It *is* vicious."

He opened the door. Joe felt he was owed a final dig.

"By the way, er, Maurice. You never said why you came."

"Didn't I? I must have mentioned it. Golf. That was it, surely I said? I thought you might fancy a round later, but I reckon you'll be occupied today, eh? Some other time."

"It'll be a pleasure. 'Bye," said Joe, closing the door and leaning against it.

"Maggie," he said, "you were magnificent! Perfect timing!"

"It should have been," she answered. "I'd been

listening at the door ever since he came in. It might have been a woman!"

Joe looked at her sternly.

"You mean when you made your full frontal revelation at the door, you *knew* bloody Maurice was in here?"

She laughed loudly.

"Supporting evidence, love. These policemen love it! You're not jealous?"

"No," said Joe thoughtfully. "As long as it's the last time. *And* the first time."

"Oh yes. Though not for any want of trying on his part. That's what made it so convincing."

"I hope," said Joe, staring out of the window at the beautifully empty street below, "I hope he remains convinced."

"If he doesn't," said Maggie, "I'll just have to let him have another look."

She ran shrieking into the bedroom as Joe advanced with a mad gleam in his eyes.

CHAPTER VII

The affair at Averingerett produced headlines in the newspapers for a couple of days. It was projected by most of them as a triumph for the police and a new manifestation of the old aristocratic virtues.

Lord Trevigore appeared on film in the television news and made a magnificent impression. He had everything an old English lord should have, white hair, piercing eyes, a noble nose, great charm, the voice of a Shakespearian actor and the inanity of a Wodehousian earl. The talk-shows, culture-corners and panel-games were soon clamouring for his services.

One of the delightful things about him, declared one producer in the *Radio Times*, was his tremendous technical interest in television, particularly the video-tape and instant replay equipment. It was believed he was setting up his own studio, for experimental purposes, at Averingerett.

From all this Joe gathered that not only had Chubb succeeded in destroying the film, but Trevigore had used the confusion caused by the fire-alarm to dispose of any other evidence which might be used against him.

The picture of the evening that came across was of a top-people's dinner-party, disturbed by an attempted burglary which the police were summoned to deal with. Lord Trevigore was enthusiastic in his praise of the police and spoke out strongly in favour of bringing back the rope, the cat, and the birch, and hinted support for the knife in the case of sexual offenders.

The police received his praise with modesty and restraint.

Chubb's fire had damaged nothing more than a section of floor and a couple of wall panels in the cupboard off the gallery. As for the lions, they were hardly mentioned at all, except by Trevigore on the telly, who slipped in plugs for the attractions of Averingerett as often as possible.

It was remarkable, Joe felt, how quickly he himself slipped back into the old routine of his life. His feelings of uneasiness wore off within forty-eight hours. School was just the same, Cyril as obsessed with travel problems as ever, Onions as nastily arrogant, Vernon as Celtic-ly cynical, Mickey Carter as adolescently malevolent, and Maisie Uppadine as pectorally superb.

As an engaged man, discretion demanded the abandonment of the Maisie-poem, but art would not be denied. It had to be finished before it could be forgotten.

He finished it early one evening, laboriously typed out a fair copy, and read it through, nodding with satisfaction at the last stanza.

Then live with me and be my love
And all our days and nights shall prove,
Whatever lying poets claim
Of modern doll or ancient dame,
(Diana, Venus, Welch, Monroe,
Whose charms may swell till they o'er flow)
THE BIGGEST TITS I'VE EVER SEEN
BELONG TO MAISIE UPPADINE.

He went into the kitchen to pour a celebratory drink. When he returned, Maggie, now the possessor of his spare key, was standing over his desk, reading the poem with great interest.

"*Ars gratia artis*," he said. "Purely aesthetic. A platonic interest in the forms of beauty."

"So I see," Maggie said. "And this is your considered opinion, is it?"

She waved the sheet of paper at him.

"No. Yes. Well, the thing is, she *rhymes*, doesn't she? And you don't." He looked at her speculatively, thinking of his mother's still-to-be-tested reaction to *Cohen*. "You wouldn't think of changing your name to Uppadine, would you? It'd only be for a few weeks, till the wedding."

"Certainly not. What's wrong with Cohen anyway? Ti-tum-ti-tum I've ever *known* belong to lovely Maggie *Cohen*. How's that?"

"I'd need to examine the claims of your *ti-tum-ti-tum* at length," he said.

"No time now," she answered, moving round the desk out of his way. "You don't want to keep Cess waiting, do you?"

No. No. Whatever else he had put behind him in the past couple of weeks, he had not lost his instinctive awe of Cess. There had been no contact at all with any member of the gang since the affair and Joe had begun to hope his liaison with the underworld was going to fade quietly away. But suddenly the summons had come, a simple phone call from Lord Jim, giving time and place of the meeting. No more. When Joe tried to question him, the phone went dead.

He told Maggie, who had been with him at the time. To his surprise she had urged that he keep the appointment.

In addition, she insisted she was coming along herself.

The rendezvous was in the usual pub. Joe parked the VW in the car-park and they found Lord Jim waiting for them just inside the door. He expressed no surprise at seeing Maggie, but held the saloon door open for her.

"We'll be through in a minute," he said. Maggie went in without demur, rather to Joe's surprise, while Jim steered him into the public-bar.

"Hello, Joe," said Cess.

"Hello, Cess," replied Joe looking uneasily at the brutal face before him. He had experienced one or two qualms lest Cess should somehow have decided he was to blame for the balls-up at Averingerett. But the man looked friendly enough. In fact, if anything, he looked more conciliatory than Joe had ever seen him before.

"How are the others?" Joe asked.

"Bertie's gone back south. The other two are keeping low for a bit. Have a drink."

Over their beer, the story of Cess's escape came out. He too had seen the opportunity offered by the confusion. They had clambered down from the roof after the lions had made their dramatic appearance, and got out simultaneously with the fire-engines' coming in. Their journey home had been a lot easier than Joe's and Jim's as Killer had still been waiting in the exchange car at the pre-arranged spot.

"But the alarm, who set the alarm off?" asked Joe, ignoring a warning tap from Jim's foot under the table.

"Me!" said Cess challengingly. "Me," he echoed gloomily. "We were on our way back when I saw this old dagger on the wall. Nothing much. Didn't seem worth enough for anyone to fix an alarm to it. I thought Mickey would like it, you know how kids like that sort of thing. So I pulled it down. And all hell broke loose!"

He sipped his drink despondently.

"It was lucky in a way," said Joe comfortingly. "It helped me and Jim out of a tough spot."

"Yeah," said Cess, without much conviction. "That's one way of looking at it. Not everybody's though. Not by a long chalk."

"So you got nothing out?"

"Not a bloody sausage. Nor you, says Jim."

"No," Joe remembered his precious book. He'd had it in his hand when they scrambled through the window. It must be lying in the garden somewhere. He hoped it would be found.

"We dumped our stuff in Chubb's room," he added. "Aye. Luckily he got to it before the police, and shifted it somewhere else to be found."

"So it was all for nothing."

"Nothing!" Cess laughed bitterly. *"Nothing!* Except what it costs to set up something like this. A small bloody fortune, that's what it's cost. *Nothing!"*

There was a long silence. They finished their drinks.

"Well," said Joe finally, "if that's our business done, I'll get back to Maggie."

He began to rise.

"Wait," said Cess. Not a command, more of a plea, thought Joe amazed. "What I really wanted to ask you Joe, is . . . well, Mrs. Carter, my wife, she's leaving me."

Joe sat down with a thump.

"I'm sorry," he said. "But I don't see . . ."

It was true. He didn't see. Either what he could do; or, for that matter, why Cess should be so upset. Surely he must have known for some time he'd been stretching their relationship to its limits?

"I'm sorry," he repeated. "She'll be taking the boy?"

"Aye," said Cess dully. "That's what I thought . . . I mean, I wondered if you'd have a word with her, tell her it would be bad for the boy, like. Us splitting up. She might listen to you, she thinks a lot of you."

This was the last thing Joe had expected to happen. He was totally unprepared and could think of nothing to say. Except perhaps that, on the surface, it seemed the wisest move Mrs. Carter had ever made.

But, despite this present evidence of Cess's humanity, he was not yet brave enough to say that.

"If you think it would be any good . . ." he said hesitantly.

"Thanks, Joe," said Cess fervently. "I'd be very much obliged. Here, look. This is for your trouble."

He pushed an envelope into Joe's hands. It contained a bundle of bank-notes.

"Look here," said Joe, "I don't want paid for doing it . . ."

"No, lad," said Carter. "That's for your work on the job. It's nowt compared to what we expected. But you were promised payment and you deserve something. Say no more. Just talk to the old lady, do your best."

He stood up, more like himself again.

"And talking of ladies, let's get through into the saloon and see what's what."

He strode on ahead aggressively, Jim and Joe following at a more sedate pace.

"Jim," said Joe. "That night after we got back. You went outside again and said something to a chap in a blue Cortina. Who was it? I'd begun to think it was the police."

"No," said Jim. "Private detectives."

"God! But why? Who'd want to watch me?"

"Not you. Alice. Though it might have involved **you**. It was her husband's notion. After divorce evidence."

"Her husband! I had forgotten she was married."

"Aye. Any road, I spoke to him. He saw reason."

He smacked his hands lightly together.

"I don't doubt it," said Joe with a shudder. "Thanks."

Jim looked at him unwinkingly.

"Not for you," he said. "For Alice. I look after them as is going to work for me."

"Alice is going to work for you?" asked Joe incredulously.

"Well, not for me," said Lord Jim. "A business acquaintance. Runs an escort service. Legit. High class."

He glared at Joe as though challenging contradiction.

"I'm sure," said Joe. Something rang a bell here. "You mean like the one Cyn works for?"

"That's it. Same one. Me, I just see there's no trouble. From no one. I mentioned it to Alice after . . ."

"After you had my supper," Joe completed.

"Right," said Lord Jim with one of his rare smiles. "She were quite interested. Nice work, meet lots of people, bit of spare cash. Your girl, Maggie, think she'd be interested?"

"No," said Joe, hurriedly. "She's really very anti-social."

"Pity," said Jim. "Nice girl. She could do well."

I'm sure she could, thought Joe looking at Jim with fascinated horror. It had been amusing to think of him finding it difficult to cope with Alice's needs. But the little man had turned the tables nicely. It was the first principle of capitalism. Take what you need for yourself, then flog what's left to those who find it hard to get hold of! He hoped Alice knew what she was doing.

They had paused to finish their conversation in the passageway between the two bars. Now the saloon door was pushed open and Cess stuck his head out.

"Come on, you two. Get a move on! Are you going to stand there yakking all day?"

He held the door open to let them pass. Joe half expected what he was going to see, but the actual sight was no less a shock to his system.

Sitting together round a table like old friends were three women who, as far as he was concerned, possessed one significant common denominator.

Maggie and Alice and Cynthia.

"Hello, Joe," said Cynthia.

"Hello, Joe," said Alice.

"Hello, Joe," said Maggie. "We were just talking about you."

The last time he had felt like this, Joe recalled, he had been facing the lions of Averingerett.

There were two more women to face before he could relax.

The first was Mrs. Carter. She listened to him stonily as he stumbled through a lot of nonsense about Cess turning over a new leaf and the importance of parental harmony at this stage in a boy's development. Her only interruption came when he made a passing reference to other women.

"Women!" she said scornfully. "You don't think this has owt to do with that Cynthia cow!"

Joe was ready to believe her. It had seemed very odd to him that the Cess and Cyn relationship was still going strong even when Carter was so distressed at the prospect of losing his wife.

Joe finished what he had to say and stood up to go. He had no hope of success, but the knowledge that Cess might be somewhere in the house, even listening, made him try a final parting shot.

"I don't think he's altogether a bad man, Mrs. Carter," he said. "Out of your influence he'd be really lost, whereas at the moment I think he's learned a lesson and will be that much more ready to do what you consider best for you all."

To his surprise his words seemed to be having some effect.

"Mebbe," she said. "I suppose I am responsible in a way. All right. I'll talk to him, I can't say fairer. And thank you for coming."

Cess was standing in the hall, smiling broadly. He'd almost certainly been listening.

"Thanks, Joe," he whispered and went in to his wife.

Joe let himself out, realized after a few steps he'd left his raincoat in the hall and silently re-entered the house to collect it.

He could hear voices from the living-room.

"How was I to know the bloody thing'd be wired?"

"Know? You're not supposed to know nowt unless I tell you! You just *do*, Cess. That's all. Just *do*!"

"But it weren't my fault the police had come!"

"Oh no," snarled Mrs. Carter. "It's never your fault, is it? Four years I've kept you out of gaol, living comfortably. A little bit here, a little bit there. Then you start getting fancy ideas! Doing the school was daft enough in itself. But doing it while I was setting up the Averingerett job were bloody stupid!"

"I wasn't nicked," said Cess surlily.

"Only because I dumped the stuff in the river.

Then you go off by yourself and nearly get nicked at the house."

"We were doing a recce," protested Cess. "I thought you'd be pleased."

"Pleased? You've done nowt to please me since you last got sent down. Listen to me, Cess. I don't mind your drinking and I don't mind your fancy woman. They can come in useful at times even. But when you start *thinking*, you and me had best part ways. If I take you back now, it's the last time. Do you understand me? By yourself you're nowt, you know that, don't you? That's the only reason you come crawling. You know that, don't you?"

"Aye," said Cess dully. "I know it."

Shaken, Joe left the house, and all the way home he tried to rearrange the words to mean something different. But in the end he had to settle for the suspicion, dark almost to the point of certainty, that he had been instrumental in repairing a union which neither God nor the law would have wept to see permanently sundered.

The second woman was his mother.

"Mam, this is Maggie. Maggie Cohen."

"Cohen? Cohen? You any relation to Allie Cohen who keeps the betting shops up in Ilford?"

"He's a cousin of my father's, I think, Mrs. Askern."

"Is he now? Well, he's a lovely kind of man, I can tell you that. Why didn't you tell me she was a relative to Allie Cohen, Joe? I don't know what you can see in him, Maggie, I'm sure I don't. He's been a bother to me since the day he was born. Such a weak, puling child I've never seen! You just got to look at the pictures to see . . . Joe, don't just stand there. Fetch the pictures!"

"Yes, Joe. Why don't you fetch the pictures?" said Maggie.

Sergeant Prince fetched the pictures a couple of weeks before the end of term.

"Wedding present," he said in answer to Joe's raised eyebrows.

"But you've given us those towels already," protested Joe, opening the large envelope and pulling out the contents.

"Bonus," said Prince. "Bit chilly today, isn't it? Maggie coming round? I'd light a little fire. See you on the tee next Sunday!"

He left. Joe didn't see him go.

He was too busy checking that all the prints of himself and Cynthia playing all the variations on a familiar theme had the negatives attached.

"Been burning something?" sniffed Maggie when she arrived.

"Only bridges. And candles at both ends," said Joe.

"Oh. Riddles, is it? I picked this up in the hall on my way in."

She passed over a book-sized packet. Joe opened it and was unsurprised to find it contained a book. Until he looked at the book.

It was a leather-bound copy of Godwin's *Political Justice*.

There was a note with it in an almost illegible semi-literate scrawl.

Found this in yr tales and cant sell so thort you will like it as weding gif.
from
yrs truly
Jim

PS Sumone scribled on sum pages but I managed to rub most out with ink ruber and its hardly to be seen now.

"What's the matter, Joe?" asked Maggie. "Why are you laughing like that?"

It was nearly the end of term. Another few days and he'd be married.

The afternoon had drifted by pleasantly in the school TV room, where in the company of 4S he had been watching Lord Trevigore introducing various aspects of Averingerett in the *Our Heritage* series. There had been a great deal of public sympathy lately for the noble lord when his son, the Hon. Julian, after being convicted on a drugs charge, had made a statement to the press condemning the hidebound, repressed, reactionary attitudes of everyone older than himself, and left for a hippy commune in Morocco.

Lord Trevigore was finishing off.

"Recently," he said, "persons unknown attempted to steal some of the lovely things I have shown you. That was wicked. Very wicked. But just as wicked are these persons, some of them not unknown, who will try to steal from all of us our old ways of life, whatever these may be. Averingerett and places like it belong to us all. The things which happened there in the past have helped to make us all what we are in the present. Never forget that. I love to come up to the old house for a bit of spiritual refreshment when I feel jaded by my duties in the House of Lords. I hope all of you who are watching will also find time to come and share what all our ancestors have left in trust for us there."

The magnificent face faded away and mixed to

the even more magnificent western façade of the house as the credit titles rolled.

Joe drew the curtains and let the sun stream in. The children yawned as if roused from sleep. In many cases they probably had been.

"Is he right when he says it's all ours?" asked Joe.

"No!" said fat Alf Certes. "It's all his, isn't it? Lord Teeveegore's."

It was a nice name. Joe smiled to himself.

"Please, sir, what do you think?" asked little Molly Jarvis, whose love for him had survived even the shock of his engagement to Maggie.

"I think it belongs to us," he said gently.

"Why do we have to pay to get in then?" snarled Mickey Carter.

"Everything has to be paid for, Carter. Though some things have been paid for a long long time ago by people quite different from us."

"Don't you ever get sick of it, sir?" asked Maisie Uppadine, whose curves had seemed to grow fuller day by day during this long, hot summer.

"Sick of what?" inquired Joe.

"Averingerett. You're there such a lot, aren't you?"

"Well, Maisie," said Joe thoughtfully. "There was a time quite recently when I did feel a bit sick of it. I didn't know if I'd ever bother to go there again. But I've got over that I think. Watching the programme this afternoon helped. Listening to Lord Trevigore convinced me. I think I ought to go there again. Yes. I really do."

The children were giggling. He turned to find Maggie smiling at him through the glass panel of the door.

His heart gave a little leap at the sight. Another fortnight and they'd be married.

She deserved the very best of life.

Possibly Lord Jim felt that the girls at the escort agency deserved the best money could buy too.

And doubtless even Cess felt that Cyn had some claim on life's goodies.

There was another PTA meeting later in the week.

Perhaps it was time he had a serious talk with Mrs. Carter.

About the Author

Reginald Hill has been widely published in both England and the United States. Among his novels are *Fell of Dark* and the famous Pascoe-Dalziel series, including *Deadheads*, *A Clubbable Woman*, and *Exit Lines* (all available in Signet). He lives with his wife in Yorkshire, England.